Bridging the Divide

By

Darryl Danford

Dedication

To my beloved family and friends, whose steadfast love and encouragement inspired every word within these pages.

Acknowledgment

I began writing this book at the age of 52 and set down the final words at 53—a journey marked by uncertainty, perseverance, some fear, and the hope that these pages would one day see the light of day.

With deepest appreciation, I wish to acknowledge the unwavering support and encouragement of my cherished family and friends. Your steadfast love has been the foundation upon which every word of this book was built. To those who have entrusted me with your stories through candid conversations, I am profoundly grateful for your honesty and openness—your journeys have shaped this work in ways beyond measure.

My sincere gratitude extends to the extraordinary doctors, nurses, and medical staff whose compassion, skill, and dedication sustained me during the creation of this book. Your expertise not only restored my health but also enabled this project to reach completion.

I am deeply grateful to my wife for her unwavering support throughout my recovery from a heart attack. Her constant encouragement, thoughtful care, and faith in my ability to finish this work gave me strength when I needed it most. Without her compassion and dedication, none of this would have been possible.

To everyone who has allowed me to be part of their journey over the years—your courage, resilience, and willingness to put the work in have been both my inspiration and my reward.

There were moments when I doubted whether I'd ever reach the final chapter. Yet, here we are, and I am profoundly grateful to have arrived at this moment, able to offer this work to the world. Each hour spent wrestling with ideas, shaping sentences, and revisiting memories has been a labor of love, made possible by the remarkable editors at House of Best Sellers, whose dedication elevated this manuscript beyond what I could have achieved alone.

To all, my heartfelt thank you.

Darryl Danford

About the Author

Six years ago, Darryl began a purposeful journey of self-development through men's groups, independent study, and intensive therapy. That work led to lasting personal growth—and a deeper calling. Since then, he has supported thousands of men in navigating their own challenges with clarity, accountability, and emotional honesty.

A retired military veteran, Darryl brings both structure and empathy to his work. His mission is to equip men with the tools to rise above hardship and lead with presence and integrity. The insights in this book are shaped by years of direct experience helping others do just that.

He currently lives in Dayton, Ohio, with his wife and their two miniature schnauzers.

Table of Contents

Introduction

We're not living in the same world our parents grew up in—and pretending we are is part of the problem.

The traditional family structure—father, mother, children under one roof—is on life support. I'm 52, and I've watched that shift firsthand. What used to be the norm is now a rarity. You don't have to like that fact, but you'd be foolish to ignore it.

This new generation was raised differently. Many were handed affirmations instead of accountability. And now we're dealing with the result: a population that struggles to handle disagreement, folds under pressure, and calls any opposing view "wrong" by default.

Disagree with someone? You're labeled problematic.

Question the narrative? You're getting canceled.

Mention that the conveniences of modern life—electricity, HVAC, transportation, infrastructure—exist largely because of male ingenuity, and watch how quickly the word "patriarchy" turns into a battle cry. The backlash doesn't come from reason. It comes from *emotion*. From identity politics. From people who've been told that any opinion that challenges theirs is a threat.

We've lost the ability to sit in tension. We've traded dialogue for outrage. And we've done it under the illusion of fairness.

Let me be blunt: equality of outcome doesn't exist. That's not opinion—it's fact.

Thomas Sowell laid it out perfectly in *Social Justice Fallacies*. He pointed out that firstborn children are significantly more likely to earn merit-based scholarships than their younger siblings. Not because they're more deserving. Not because they had more love or better schools. Just because of how life works.

Same household. Same parents. Same rules. Yet firstborns win more often.

Why? No one really knows. Maybe it's prenatal development. Maybe it's attention dynamics. Maybe it's pressure or expectation. Doesn't matter. The outcome is what it is—and it's not "fair" by the modern definition. But it is real.

I've seen it in my own family. My sister, my brother, and I all grew up under the same roof, with the same parents. But we're not the same. Not in how we think, not in how we live, and not in the outcomes we've each created. That's not dysfunction. That's human nature.

Each person processes life differently. Each person makes choices. And while wisdom can be shared, it can't be forced. You can hand two kids the same playbook—what they do with it is on them.

This book isn't about trying to fix the world. It's about calling out the nonsense, offering some clarity, and reminding people that personal responsibility still matters. If you're looking for sugar-coated takes and soft landings, you're in the wrong place.

But if you're ready to take ownership of your life, your relationships, and your standards—keep reading.

Because the truth is still worth hearing.

Let me break it down.

You can grow up in the same household as your siblings, sit at the same dinner table, face the same discipline, and still come out with entirely different takeaways. That's not dysfunction. That's human perception.

When my sister and I compare notes about our childhood, it's clear we didn't experience it the same way. If our father yelled at us over something one of us did, we both absorbed it differently. Maybe one of us saw it as discipline. Maybe the other internalized it as shame. The facts were the same—the impact wasn't.

That's the point: it's not just what happens to you—it's what you take from it.

People carry different lessons from the same moment, because each person brings their own lens to the experience. That's why two people raised under one roof can grow up with opposite values, beliefs, and behavior patterns.

This isn't just about childhood—it applies to every aspect of life, especially when it comes to relationships between men and women.

Some women were taught how to treat a man—with respect, clarity, and emotional maturity. Others weren't. Their examples came from broken homes, bitter mothers, or a culture that taught them that men are disposable.

Same goes for men. Some were taught how to show up for a woman—how to listen, lead, protect, and provide.

Others were left to figure it out through trial, error, and YouTube videos.

No two people see things the same way. And when you bring in the weight of social constructs—politics, patriarchy, feminism, masculinity, race, justice—the divide gets even wider. People hear the same word and react with completely different emotions based on their upbringing, media exposure, and personal pain.

So let me say something that won't sit well with everyone, and that's fine with me.

Third-wave feminism has gone off the rails.

What started as a movement to support and empower women has, in many circles, become a weapon used to vilify men. It's no longer about equality—it's about blame. It's about tearing men down to lift women up, which isn't empowerment. It's revenge wrapped in victimhood.

You don't have to agree with that. I'm not asking you to. But I'm not going to pretend I don't believe it either. I've seen it. I've lived it. And I've watched good men be unfairly labeled because they didn't bend to a narrative they never agreed to in the first place.

Let me be clear: I'm not denying that there are men out there doing and saying foolish, even harmful, things about women. There are. But let's not pretend it doesn't happen in reverse.

There are women out there using their pain as a license to humiliate, manipulate, and disrespect men. You see it online. You hear it in conversations. You feel it in the double standards we're expected to tolerate without pushing back.

I've learned the hard way that being a good man doesn't exempt you from being targeted. And once the label sticks, no one wants to hear your side. You're just lumped in with the worst of us.

That's the reality. You can either get bitter or you can get clear.

And this book is about clarity.

Scroll through mainstream media, YouTube, or just about any social platform, and you'd think men and women flat-out hate each other.

I don't buy that. Not for a second.

What we're seeing isn't reality—it's a carefully curated, emotionally charged narrative designed to divide and profit. Because let's be honest: conflict gets clicks. Outrage fuels algorithms. And people making money off your attention have zero incentive to show you anything healthy, constructive, or nuanced.

So here's the truth: what you see online is not an accurate reflection of how men and women actually feel about each other. It's a distorted highlight reel of worst-case scenarios, toxic extremes, and one-sided grievances.

Hating the opposite sex is not the norm—it's the noise.

But the internet does a damn good job of amplifying that noise. You get a few loud voices on either side, and suddenly it feels like a war. Men saying all women are manipulative. Women saying all men are trash. And right in the middle, the rest of us—trying to have real conversations—get drowned out.

You'll even see men defending destructive behavior from women just to win favor or avoid conflict. They're often labeled "white knights." And while they're not the majority, they're loud enough online to seem like they represent all of us.

But ask yourself: how much of this is actually true? How much of what you're seeing is reality—and how much is just performance?

Let me make something clear, in case it needs to be said: I'm not calling women liars. I'm not calling men liars either.

What I'm saying is that truth usually lives somewhere in the middle. And we'd be foolish not to acknowledge that.

Some people—regardless of gender—just aren't good people. That's not deep. That's not controversial. That's just real. And pretending otherwise doesn't help anyone.

If you're going to be in a relationship—one worth keeping—both of you need to put down the sword.

Stop fighting each other and start examining the dynamic you're creating together. Healthy relationships aren't built by winning arguments or proving points. They're built by two emotionally mature people willing to hold a mirror to themselves and take responsibility.

That goes for both men and women. Equally.

If the things I've said so far resonate with you, then understand this:

You can't build something strong by focusing on who's to blame.

You build it by focusing on what needs to be better—and what role you're playing in making it worse.

That's not soft talk. That's truth.

I believe in every word I've written here. If that makes me the one who has to say it out loud, so be it. Someone needs to stop tiptoeing around the obvious and finally put it on paper.

That's what this book is doing.

I'm past the point of caring who disagrees or takes offense. I'm not here to please everyone. I'm here to say what I know to be true—and if it challenges you, good. Growth never starts in comfort.

Men and women need to put down the weapons, both in how we treat each other publicly and how we interact privately in our relationships.

Yes, there will always be men who mistreat the women they're with. Just like there will always be women who mock, disrespect, or resent the men in their lives. That's not new, and it's not gender-exclusive. It's about character, not chromosomes.

And yet, with age and perspective, I've seen this too: Many women eventually reflect on the men in their lives—their fathers, brothers, exes—and realize they were doing the best they could with what they knew at the time. That recognition comes late for some. Too late for others.

There are women I've known, women and relationships that I reflect on. Not because I was perfect, quite the contrary. But because we're all just human, trying to figure it out while carrying the baggage we didn't ask for.

None of us are entirely good or bad. We're flawed. We're evolving. And we each carry our own set of values, needs, and expectations into every relationship.

There's nothing wrong with having standards. In fact, there's something deeply wrong with not having them.

And just because you've been hurt doesn't mean you abandon the whole idea of love. Just because you've seen the worst of someone doesn't mean the opposite sex is the enemy. That kind of thinking will rob you of everything real.

We were designed—intended—to connect. You don't have to be religious to understand that. Men and women are wired to complement each other. Not perfectly. Not without friction. But with purpose.

That's why I wrote this book.

Not to complain. Not to vent. Not to stir the pot. But to offer a perspective on how real relationships actually work when people stop pretending and start owning who they are.

I'm not here to fix society. I'm here to remind you of what still matters:

- Self-respect
- Clear standards
- Personal accountability
- And most of all, the ability to treat each other with respect, honesty, love, and empathy

Because when we get that part right, everything else has a chance to work.

Chapter 1:
Breaking Down the Divide:
The Changing Dynamics of Men, Women, and Relationships

"If you cannot achieve equality of performance among people born to the same parents and raised under the same roof, how realistic is it to expect to achieve equality of outcomes across broader and deeper social divisions?"

– Thomas Sowell

Before we talk about how men and women are missing the mark in relationships today, we need to zoom out. There's a much bigger issue at play—and it's been brewing for decades.

Masculinity and femininity haven't just been questioned—they've been under attack. This isn't just a personal identity crisis. It's an erosion of the very structure that once held families together. And when we lose touch with those core identities, everyone pays the price.

Feminism, in its original form, had a purpose I respect. It was about equal opportunity. Leveling the playing field. Giving women access to rights, roles, and resources they'd been denied for too long.

But the version we're seeing today? It's morphed into something else entirely. This new brand of feminism isn't about equality anymore—it's about superiority. It's become a movement that often aims to diminish men, not elevate women.

The word "patriarchy" gets thrown around like a weapon. Masculinity is labeled toxic by default. And there's this growing narrative that men—especially straight, masculine men—have nothing meaningful to offer. That's not empowerment. That's division.

And it's getting louder.

I recently watched a clip from a Taylor Swift concert where she shouted, *"Fuck* the patriarchy," and the crowd roared in response. It was performative. It was loud. And it was misguided.

Because let's call it what it is: the mic in her hand? Engineered by men. The sound system blasting her voice through the arena? Designed by men. The light rigging, the power infrastructure, the venue itself—all built by men. And those concert tickets bought by teenage girls? More often than not, paid for by fathers, brothers, or boyfriends who just want their loved ones to smile.

So when someone with that level of influence shouts something like that, what message does it send?

It teaches young women—many still forming their worldview—that men are the enemy. That masculinity is oppressive. That the people they'll rely on in life are part of some abstract problem that needs to be dismantled.

But here's the truth: most men aren't the enemy. And most women aren't out to destroy men either. But these messages are driving a wedge where unity and respect should exist. And if we keep letting that wedge get driven deeper, we're going to keep creating fractured families, bitter relationships, and broken communication between the sexes.

Words matter. Narratives matter. When phrases like "patriarchy" get tossed around without context, they lose meaning—and create confusion, not clarity. They replace dialogue with hostility. They rob both men and women of the ability to see each other clearly.

If we want to fix what's broken between us, we've got to stop fighting shadows and start confronting the real issues—together.

Let's get something straight: it's not a man's world anymore. Not by a long shot.

Yes, men still build a large share of the world's infrastructure. They engineer the tech, drive the logistics, and fuel the industries that keep modern life running. But look beyond the surface, and the picture isn't nearly as dominant as some would like to believe.

Men are struggling—and most people aren't talking about it.

Men die by suicide at a significantly higher rate than women. They're incarcerated more frequently, and when convicted of the same crimes, they often receive harsher sentences. The education gap has flipped, too. What was once a male-dominated domain now shows men statistically trailing women in graduation rates and academic achievement.

But here's the part that gets swept under the rug: what kind of education are we even talking about?

Particularly in younger liberal circles, there's a concerning pattern—conformity disguised as education. I've watched it happen on college campuses, where intellectual curiosity used to thrive. Now, you step on the wrong ideological nerve, and the room goes cold. Debate is out. Echo chambers are in.

That kind of groupthink doesn't just impact students—it spills into relationships. Into marriages. Into workplaces. When we raise a generation that confuses opinion for truth and silences disagreement with labels, we're not building strong women or strong men. We're breeding fragility and friction.

This isn't a swipe at women. It's a challenge to the culture we've created around education and identity. And it matters—especially when it comes to how men and women relate to one another.

Let's look at another piece of the puzzle that rarely gets discussed: the lack of male teachers, especially in primary and secondary education.

Think about the impact that has. Young boys go through their most formative years, rarely seeing a man in a position of mentorship or authority in the classroom. Girls grow up without seeing how emotionally intelligent, grounded men engage in nurturing roles. We lose perspective. We lose balance.

But we don't fix this by pointing fingers. The truth is, men aren't choosing teaching. And we need to ask why.

Maybe it's because teaching has been painted as a "feminine" profession. Maybe it's the low pay, the lack of respect, or the perception that success means chasing bigger money in tech, finance, or engineering. Whatever the reason, we've created a stigma around one of the most important roles in society—and both boys and girls are paying the price.

Now let's flip the coin.

While women dominate public education, men dominate another space—one that's growing louder and more dangerous by the day: male-centered media platforms.

I'm talking about certain websites, podcasts, forums, and influencers who claim to speak for men but spend more time bashing women than building men. They frame women as problems. They reduce relationships to power struggles. They call it "truth," but all they're doing is channeling bitterness into branding.

Don't get me wrong—men need space to talk about male issues. That's healthy. But when the tone turns bitter and the message becomes "us vs. them," all we're doing is creating a mirror image of the extreme feminism we claim to hate.

That's not masculinity. That's just trauma in disguise.

If you're building yourself up by tearing women down, you're not growing—you're projecting.

What men need—and what women need, too—is not more outrage. It's more honesty. More accountability. More structure. More clarity.

Less blaming. More building.

The absence of strong male role models in education and the rise of toxic male-focused media platforms have created a dangerous feedback loop.

Young men go through school without ever seeing a grounded, emotionally mature man in a position of influence. They don't witness strength combined with empathy. They don't learn how real masculinity functions in leadership. So when they go looking for answers later in life, they often find the wrong voices waiting for them.

Instead of wisdom, they find rage.

Instead of leadership, they find bitterness.

Instead of guidance, they find echo chambers telling them women are the enemy.

And the problem gets worse from there.

If we're serious about building healthier relationships between men and women, we need to amplify voices that call for mutual respect and understanding. Not voices that fuel animosity for clicks. Not platforms that masquerade as male empowerment while reinforcing resentment.

Because this isn't just about media content or career choices—it's about the messages we normalize and the long-term impact they have on the next generation.

Now, I'll be fair. Some of these so-called male-centered podcasts and platforms offer nuggets of truth. They say some things that deserve to be heard. But you can't ignore the rest of it—the twisted narratives, the coded language, the subtle contempt dressed up as confidence.

Shows that refer to women as "304s"—a thinly veiled substitute for "hoes"—aren't offering insight. They're peddling shame.

Shows that repeatedly ask women "What do you bring to the table?" without any real intent to listen aren't fostering dialogue. They're picking a fight.

That question *could* be valuable in a real conversation between two emotionally mature adults. But most of the time, it's framed to belittle, not build. It's meant to put women on trial, not invite them into a relationship built on clarity and mutual benefit.

And make no mistake—this mindset is doing damage.

It's turning men and women into competitors, not companions.

It's building up emotional walls where there should be understanding.

It's making connection harder to achieve because both sides walk in expecting war instead of alignment.

But here's the deeper problem—and it's one nobody wants to admit:

We've lost touch with the wisdom of the generations before us.

There used to be a time when phrases like "back in my day" actually meant something. Older generations passed down values, principles, and lessons. They weren't perfect, but they offered *continuity*. A sense of how relationships work when both people understand sacrifice, structure, and shared responsibility.

That language has started to disappear.

Not because the past was flawless. But because today's society has made anything traditional seem outdated, oppressive, or irrelevant. Now we act like the past has nothing to teach us—like there's no value in how our parents and grandparents stayed together for decades, raised families, and fought for each other instead of against each other.

And as a result, we're disconnected—not just from each other, but from the core values that held us together in the first place.

It's time to change that.

This disappearance of "back in my day" wisdom isn't just a generational gap—it's a symptom of a deeper cultural shift.

We've lost the thread that once connected one generation to the next. There's no longer a clear set of shared values or lessons being passed down. Instead, young men and women are left sifting through a minefield of mixed messages—most of which divide more than they clarify.

The result? A generation raised without a compass.

They're not learning from the past. They're drowning in ideologies that contradict each other. And when that becomes your foundation, how do you build a relationship rooted in mutual respect and understanding?

You don't. You build it on suspicion, stereotypes, and unrealistic expectations.

We've created a culture that values novelty over wisdom. And in doing so, we've told an entire generation that tradition is irrelevant. That anything rooted in the past must be outdated, harmful, or oppressive.

So when someone today tries to share a perspective shaped by experience—especially if it sounds "traditional"—they're often dismissed before they finish the sentence.

"That doesn't apply anymore."

"That's outdated thinking."

"That's not how we do it now."

It's a knee-jerk rejection of anything that reminds us how things *used* to be. But here's the problem: tradition is where many of life's most valuable insights live.

It doesn't mean we go backward. It means we stop ignoring what still works.

Tradition isn't the enemy of progress. It's the context for it. It's the hard-won knowledge of those who came before us—people who struggled, adapted, built, and raised families in a world that demanded strength, clarity, and emotional endurance. That wisdom still matters.

But today, we're so quick to toss it aside that we've created a cultural divide between those who appreciate that wisdom and those who treat it like baggage.

Rejecting tradition wholesale doesn't make us smarter. It makes us blind to what already works.

And that blindness makes it harder to grow—personally, professionally, and relationally. It makes it harder to navigate love, conflict, and purpose without stumbling into mistakes others have already made and solved.

We've told ourselves that each generation has to start over. That they need to figure everything out from scratch. But re-inventing the wheel isn't noble. It's unnecessary.

You don't have to choose between tradition and progress. The strongest foundation comes from using both—pulling from the past while moving forward with purpose.

But to do that, we have to be willing to listen.

Because if we can't respect the wisdom that came before us, we'll keep losing connection to our roots—and to each other.

And we'll keep raising men and women who are more suspicious than sincere, more reactive than reflective, and more disconnected than ever before.

These days, it feels like every breakup comes with a diagnosis.

"He was a narcissist."

"She was a crazy bitch."

It's as if we've forgotten that two grown adults can simply realize they're not a fit anymore—and leave it at that.

Somewhere along the line, we lost the ability to accept that relationships can end without assigning blame to a villain. That maybe, just maybe, two people can grow apart, change values, or wake up one day and recognize that compatibility has run its course.

But instead of admitting that, we slap on the harshest label we can find and write the other person off as "toxic."

Let me be clear—toxic behavior is real, and yes, some relationships are abusive, manipulative, or emotionally destructive. But the reality is, not every breakup is rooted in pathology. Sometimes, people just change. Sometimes, they just clash. And that's enough.

The problem with overusing terms like "narcissist" or "crazy" is that we stop learning.

We stop reflecting.

We stop taking any ownership of our side of the story.

It becomes easier to say, "They were the problem," than to ask, "What did I ignore? What role did I play? What can I learn from this?"

And that's where we lose growth.

Every time you label your ex as a psychological case study without a shred of clinical evidence, you rob yourself of clarity. You turn your pain into projection instead of introspection.

And you carry that bitterness into your next relationship.

This isn't just about avoiding blame. It's about maturity.

Relationships are complex. People are flawed. Not every failed connection needs to be painted as a war between the wounded and the wicked.

Sometimes, it's just incompatibility. Sometimes, it's evolution. And sometimes, it's just timing.

You can still walk away with dignity and self-respect without burning the other person to the ground.

Yes—real narcissism exists. So do real mental health issues. But they are not the reason for every breakup, and we've got to stop pretending they are. Most of these accusations are made out of pain, not out of diagnosis. They're reactions, not reflections.

And while it may feel good to brand your ex with a label, it won't help you heal.

If anything, it stops you from seeing the full picture—and keeps you from understanding your own patterns, blind spots, or decisions that helped shape the dynamic.

Here's a truth most people don't want to hear:

Sometimes, it's nobody's fault.

Sometimes, it just doesn't work.

And learning to accept that—with honesty and emotional intelligence—is what separates people who grow from people who repeat.

When we label every failed relationship with extreme terms, we rob ourselves of maturity.

We turn human complexity into caricature. We act like incompatibility is always a crisis, instead of what it often is—a normal, human outcome. Sometimes two people simply don't fit. That's not dysfunction. That's life.

More on this later, but let me be clear right now: not every breakup requires a villain. Sometimes walking away is about recognizing fundamental differences—not diagnosing the other person as broken.

Now let's talk about a topic most people sidestep—masculinity.

The definition of what it means to "be a man" has shifted so many times that it's hard to tell what's expected anymore. Society constantly encourages men to get in touch with their "feminine side." But when's the last time you heard someone tell a woman to get in touch with her *masculine* side?

Exactly.

This lopsided messaging has left a generation of men uncertain, passive, and sometimes paralyzed. Especially in relationships.

I've seen it too often—men giving up leadership, direction, and decisiveness because they've been told those traits are controlling, toxic, or outdated. Instead, they default to neutrality. They avoid conflict. They take a backseat and hope that being agreeable will keep the peace.

It doesn't.

Let's get something straight: mutual respect is essential. But structure and direction still matter. Relationships need clarity. They need grounding. And when a man completely relinquishes his sense of strength or decisiveness, the relationship loses its spine.

Sure, some women may appreciate the freedom that comes with leading. But over time, that freedom often turns into frustration. Because when a man stops being decisive, the relationship becomes aimless. It drifts. It loses momentum. And eventually, resentment replaces connection.

Women don't want to carry the emotional and strategic weight of a relationship alone. Even the most independent, capable women still want to feel secure in who they're with. That doesn't mean domination—it means direction. It means having a man who knows what he stands for and where he's going.

A relationship without that kind of structure becomes shaky fast.

Not because women need to be led, but because both people need to know what role they're playing—and what values they're anchoring the relationship in.

When a man suppresses his masculinity entirely, it creates confusion—for him and for her.

And confusion, over time, turns into disconnection.

At the end of the day, a healthy relationship requires structure—not surrender.

That structure comes from both people contributing their strengths—not one dominating while the other disappears. When either person takes total control, the relationship becomes unstable. Not because of power, but because the natural dynamic gets distorted.

For men, this often starts with a simple misstep: losing touch with their own masculinity.

Now let me be clear—masculinity isn't the rejection of femininity. It's the grounding force that brings strength, clarity, and stability to the relationship. Just like feminine energy brings empathy, nurturing, and intuition. When both are present—and respected—there's flow. There's equilibrium. Things click.

But when a man disowns his masculine qualities, he becomes passive, inconsistent, and often anxious. His significant other may not be able to name it, but she feels it. Something's off. Something's unanchored.

And instead of stepping up, many men start shrinking.

They stop enforcing the standards they had at the beginning of the relationship. They start making quiet concessions—giving up their time, their preferences, their voice—thinking that keeping the peace is the noble thing to do.

But that's not harmony. That's self-erasure.

It starts small. One boundary gets bent. Then another. And another.

Until one day, the man who entered the relationship with a sense of who he was—no longer recognizes himself.

That's how resentment builds. Quietly. Internally. And inevitably.

He tells himself he's doing everything he can to make it work. But she sees what he doesn't—he's lost his edge. He's lost his center. And that shift doesn't draw her closer. It pushes her away.

Because what she was once drawn to—his decisiveness, his standards, his steadiness—is now buried in passivity and attempts to make her "happy".

Now her "wants" and his "needs" are entangled in a confusing dynamic neither one fully understands. And the more he tries to please, the more she feels something's missing. Something foundational.

This is the slow decay of a relationship built on appeasement, not alignment.

The fix isn't complicated—but it does require courage:

A man must stand firm in his values.

Not in defiance, but in clarity. Not to control, but to remain authentic.

Because when both people in a relationship know exactly who they are and what they expect, mutual respect is the natural outcome. That's when understanding deepens. That's when trust solidifies. That's when things grow.

But when one person constantly bends while the other adjusts their expectations in real-time, what you're building isn't a relationship—it's a slow unraveling.

So here's the truth:

You don't save the relationship by sacrificing yourself.
You save it by showing up fully—and refusing to apologize for it.

Before the rise of the women's liberation movement in the 1960s and '70s, relationships operated under a different dynamic.

Back then, women were fighting hard for rights they'd long been denied—rights they absolutely deserved. That fight led to real progress, and no reasonable person should dismiss the sacrifices made to get there.

But fast-forward to today, and we've entered a new era—one where women now have access to virtually every opportunity that men do. Career paths, legal protections, education, leadership roles—those doors are open. Rightfully so.

So the question isn't whether women still need to fight for equality.

The question is—what happened to men in the process?

Because something's shifted. And not in a good way.

Too many men today are unanchored—unsure of themselves, unsure of their role, and unsure of how to lead within their own lives, let alone a relationship.

Our grandfathers didn't operate like that. Neither did our great-uncles nor great-grandfathers. What I call the "greater generations" had a different kind of masculinity. One rooted in resilience, responsibility, and purpose. They didn't need to perform. They just showed up.

A man's character *was* his contribution. His worth wasn't tied to optics. It was tied to consistency. He didn't need to prove himself through grand gestures or endless validation. He proved himself by getting up early, doing the hard thing, and keeping his word.

And that's what earned him loyalty. That's what built real trust.

Today? That's changed. Now men are expected to impress. Perform. Chase. Over-explain. Over-adapt. All in hopes of being "good enough" in a world that can't even define what that means anymore.

And the more they do that, the more disconnected they become—from their values, from their confidence, and from their own masculinity.

Let's be honest: in our pursuit of progress, we've also lost something.

We've lost grounding.

We've lost the principles that once gave men a clear internal compass.

We've lost the understanding that a man's worth isn't proven—it's lived.

And no, reclaiming those values doesn't mean rolling back the clock or rejecting equality. It means remembering that strength, consistency, and duty are still essential. It means teaching men to stop apologizing for being grounded in who they are—and to stop confusing appeasement for connection.

Because progress doesn't work when it comes at the cost of identity.

Let's be honest. Life used to be simpler.

People weren't constantly chasing the next trend or trying to outpace their neighbors. They weren't glued to devices, comparing their lives to strangers online. Roles were clear. Expectations were straightforward. And most families operated within a structure that—while imperfect—offered stability.

The man went to work. He provided for the household.

The woman ran the home. She raised the kids. Both had responsibilities. Both contributed. And both understood the weight of their role.

This wasn't about restriction. It was about clarity.

In that structure, the mother wasn't shackled—she was empowered. She had the freedom to raise her children in a way that aligned with the family's values. And those values were usually unified between both parents. The father, even if less hands-on day-to-day, shaped the direction. The mother reinforced it through daily nurture and presence.

Each brought something vital to the table—not competing, but complementing. That's what created a real foundation.

No, it wasn't perfect. But what it gave families—especially children—was a sense of security that's rare today. It gave kids consistency. Identity. A defined sense of who they were and what they could count on.

Contrast that with today's flexibility, and while we've certainly gained more freedom, we've also lost a lot of grounding.

Back then, submission wasn't a dirty word. It wasn't about control or weakness. It was about alignment. Trust. Mutual investment in the bigger picture.

The mother typically stayed home. The father worked a full-time job to support the family. Because her access to finances depended on what he earned, there was an unspoken contract between them—a mutual dependence built on cooperation and purpose.

He provided. She cultivated. He protected. She nurtured. And together, they built a home with shared direction.

That division of roles wasn't a power imbalance. It was a structure. And structure gave the family unit its rhythm.

We can debate the imperfections of that model all day. But what we can't deny is this:

That kind of clarity and shared responsibility built something strong.

And in today's hyper-individualized culture, we're paying the price for losing it.

Today's relationship dynamics offer more flexibility—two people can both contribute financially, both pursue careers, and both shape the household in different ways.

But in that freedom, something got lost: clarity. Purpose. Mutual dependence.

The traditional family structure may not have been perfect, but it was clear. It was built on shared responsibility—a sense that each person knew what they were showing up for and what role they were accountable to.

It worked because both people understood this simple truth: if you don't do your part, the whole thing falls apart.

And that foundation—clear expectations, shared goals, and unspoken trust—is what gave families a sense of stability.

So what kept women in those relationships? What made them stay when today's culture would scream "patriarchy" or "oppression"?

Simple: they could count on the men they were with.

Men from that era followed through. They said what they meant and backed it with action.

They didn't hide behind excuses.

They didn't procrastinate, disappear, or binge on distractions.

They took care of what they said they would take care of.

A man's word meant something. It was his bond. If he gave you a yes, it wasn't a placeholder—it was a promise. And if he failed, it wasn't from lack of effort. He showed up. He tried. He carried the weight he committed to.

That kind of man didn't need constant praise. He didn't need to be begged.

He did what was necessary—because it was necessary.

And when a woman saw that—saw the consistency, the accountability, the quiet grit—she didn't feel like a slave to the relationship. She felt like part of a team. A team where both people brought value, purpose, and trust to the table.

That's the difference.

It wasn't about control. It wasn't about power. It was about mutual investment in something bigger than either of them individually. And that mutuality created a bond that didn't need constant affirmation.

It just worked.

Because both people meant what they said, and honored what they built.

32

Chapter 2:
Understanding the Frames
Masculine and Feminine Dynamics in a
Confused Society

For relationships to truly thrive, men and women must first understand their natural tendencies and roles within the masculine and feminine frames. In my experience, these frames are not arbitrary—they are deeply rooted in the unique strengths each gender brings to the world. The masculine frame emphasizes strength, leadership, and stability, while the feminine frame centers on nurturing, emotional connection, and adaptability. These traits are not in opposition; they are complementary forces that create balance and harmony when embraced authentically.

However, I've observed that modern society has introduced a troubling level of confusion. Men are often shamed for their assertiveness, labeled as aggressive, and told to suppress their natural instincts in favor of heightened sensitivity. Meanwhile, women are celebrated for ambition and independence but discouraged from embracing their strengths in caregiving and empathy. This messaging leaves both genders disconnected from their true identities, unsure of where they fit in their relationships, families, and society.

Let's be clear—this shift hasn't just confused individuals; it's created a societal ripple effect. Men, stripped of their sense of purpose, often feel lost, frustrated, and resentful. Women, on the other hand, face the impossible pressure to "do it all," juggling career demands with the innate drive to nurture and connect emotionally. Neither gender wins in this scenario. Instead, relationships falter as people struggle to relate to one another in authentic and fulfilling ways.

Understanding these frames isn't about reverting to outdated gender roles. It's about recognizing that each frame carries inherent strengths that are critical for balanced and successful relationships. When a man provides, protects, and leads, he offers stability and direction. When a woman nurtures, empathizes, and fosters emotional depth, she creates connection and understanding. Together, these qualities form a relationship that is greater than the sum of its parts. I've seen this dynamic in action, and it's remarkable how powerful it can be when both people lean into their natural tendencies.

Restoring this balance starts with rejecting the societal narratives that pit masculinity against femininity. Men and women are not in competition—they are designed to complement one another. When we embrace this truth, the confusion and resentment that so often plague relationships begin to dissipate. Instead, we find clarity, purpose, and a shared sense of direction.

This isn't just theory; it's a call to action. Men must rediscover the strength and leadership that define their masculine frame, and women must feel empowered to fully embrace their nurturing, empathetic nature. Only then can relationships thrive. It's about creating relationships rooted in mutual respect, shared goals, and an understanding of the unique roles we are meant to play. Together, men and women can build a foundation of harmony and purpose— but it starts with embracing who we are at our core.

The Erosion of Masculinity and Its Consequences

The weakening of men carries an immense societal cost, one that doesn't stop at the individual—it ripples through families, communities, and generations. As a father myself, this concern hits close to home. When I think about my daughters, I ask myself: Who will protect and provide for them in a world where masculinity is not just discouraged but outright vilified? This isn't just a problem for men; it destabilizes the foundation of relationships and families. Historically, men have been the anchors of security and provision. When this role is diminished, the balance within relationships shifts, often creating a vacuum of responsibility and leadership.

This shift is felt most acutely by young men. They are growing up in a world that tells them their natural instincts—strength, assertiveness, and competitiveness—are problems to be fixed. Many boys, especially those from single-mother households, lack consistent male role models who can guide them through the complexities of becoming men. A father's presence—or that of a strong male mentor—is crucial. Boys need someone to show them how to channel their strength into protection, how to assert themselves without being domineering but dominant, and how to balance courage with empathy. Without this guidance, boys are left adrift, trying to decipher masculinity on their own. Too often, they turn to media or peers for answers, which leads to distorted or harmful perceptions of what it means to be a man. I've seen this firsthand in young men who feel alienated from their own identity, unsure of their role in relationships or society.

What makes this worse is the widespread demonization of masculinity. Boys are taught—sometimes explicitly, sometimes subtly—that their natural tendencies are wrong. Assertiveness is framed as aggression. Competition is labeled selfish. Strength is seen as oppressive. Let me be clear: this narrative stifles the very traits that allow boys to grow into capable, responsible men. Masculinity, at its core, is not about control or domination—it is about resilience, responsibility, and the ability to protect and provide. When society suppresses these qualities, it harms not just boys but the communities they live in. We are weakening the very foundation of stability and leadership that masculinity provides.

Biological realities reflect this erosion. The decline in testosterone levels among men is a stark indicator. Testosterone, often misunderstood as simply the "aggression hormone," is critical for male development. It drives competitiveness, physical strength, and a willingness to take risks—qualities that, when balanced, are invaluable. Yet modern lifestyles, coupled with societal pressures to suppress aggression and competitiveness, have contributed to this decline, particularly among young men. The implications are profound: lower energy levels, diminished confidence, and a decreased sense of purpose. I've spoken to men who feel like they've lost their edge, and I can tell you—it's not just in their heads. It's real, and it's a crisis.

Then there's the media. Campaigns like Gillette's ad on "toxic masculinity" may have had good intentions, but they sent the wrong message. By painting aggression and competition—core aspects of masculinity—as inherently negative, they alienated the very group they aimed to inspire. Aggression, when channeled constructively, is not only natural but necessary. It's how boys learn to stand up for themselves, defend others, and navigate conflict. These experiences are crucial for building confidence and resilience. To rob boys of these opportunities is to deny them the tools they need to become strong, capable men.

Physical play, competition, and even occasional conflict are essential in a boy's journey toward manhood. These aren't just "roughhousing" or moments of chaos; they are opportunities for boys to learn how to set boundaries, assert their presence, and respect others. If we stifle this process, we leave boys ill-equipped to handle the challenges of adulthood. Masculinity, when expressed healthily, is not a threat—it's a cornerstone of stability. It's time society recognized this truth.

**Encouraging boys to embrace their natural tendencies doesn't mean letting them run wild. It means guiding them toward responsibility and empathy while allowing them to explore the qualities that make them strong. This is the balance we need to restore. As a father, as a coach, as someone who cares deeply about the future, I believe we can rewrite this narrative. But it starts with rejecting the false notion that masculinity is a problem. Instead, we must see it for what it truly is: a vital, stabilizing force that benefits us all.

Boys Need to Be Boys

Boys need the freedom to face their challenges and navigate conflicts on their own. I've seen time and time again that when boys are overly shielded, they struggle to develop the tools they need to handle life's inevitable difficulties. This isn't just about fostering independence; it's about preparing them for adulthood. When we step in at every sign of conflict, even with the best intentions, we rob boys of the chance to build critical skills like problem-solving, resilience, and confidence. They begin to rely on authority figures to fix their problems rather than learning to trust their instincts and capabilities.

Interventionist parenting, though often driven by love and a desire to protect, can create adults who lack the mental and emotional fortitude to handle adversity. Resilience isn't something you can teach through lectures or advice alone—it has to be earned through experience. When boys are denied the opportunity to figure things out for themselves, they miss out on crucial moments of growth. Struggles, mistakes, and even outright failures are not setbacks; they're stepping stones. These experiences teach boys to think critically, adapt to changing circumstances, and push forward despite difficulty. I've coached enough young men to know that those who've faced challenges head-on are far better equipped to succeed later in life.

Allowing boys to handle their own conflicts is especially vital when it comes to social hierarchies and relationships. Hierarchies are a natural part of human interaction, and boys often learn to navigate them through play, competition, and occasional disputes. What might look like minor squabbles on the playground to an adult are, for boys, microcosms of the real-world challenges they'll face as men. Through these interactions, they learn how to assert themselves, negotiate with others, and lead when necessary. At the same time, they begin to understand the importance of empathy, compromise, and accountability in resolving disagreements.

That said, I'm not suggesting a completely hands-off approach. Common sense always has to prevail. If a child's physical safety or emotional well-being is at serious risk, stepping in is the right thing to do. But not every disagreement requires intervention. When two boys are establishing their positions in a social hierarchy or working through a nonviolent conflict, stepping back and letting them navigate the situation often yields the best outcomes. These are teachable moments, and boys need the space to learn from them.

This process isn't about fairness or ensuring equality of outcome—it's about preparing boys for the realities of life. The earlier they understand that life isn't always fair, the better prepared they'll be to face adulthood. Masculinity thrives in a world of wins and losses, not in a world where everyone gets a participation trophy. This truth might seem harsh to some, but it shapes how men approach challenges, relationships, and opportunities. Boys who grasp this early develop the resilience and drive necessary to thrive in competitive environments.

Parents and educators play a crucial role here. It's essential to make boys feel supported and loved, but that doesn't mean shielding them from every hardship. Let them experience discomfort, conflict, and failure. These moments, though challenging in the short term, are invaluable in the long run. They teach boys to trust their instincts, rely on their strengths, and navigate relationships with confidence and maturity. I've worked with young men who struggled because they were overprotected, and I've worked with others who thrived because they were given room to fail and learn. The difference is striking.

As parents, mentors, and teachers, we need to step back at times. When we allow boys to face their challenges, we empower them to grow into capable, self-assured men who can handle whatever life throws their way. Trust me— letting boys be boys isn't about neglecting them. It's about setting them up for a future where they can stand tall, face adversity, and succeed.

The Myth of Equity in Masculinity

In today's culture, equity has become a buzzword—a seemingly noble idea that promises everyone will end up in the same place, regardless of effort, skill, or circumstances. On the surface, it sounds like fairness, but I've seen how its application undermines the principles that truly drive personal and societal growth. The obsession with equal outcomes is fundamentally at odds with the essence of masculinity, which thrives on competition, risk-taking, and the relentless pursuit of excellence. Masculinity isn't about guaranteeing results for everyone; it's about striving, overcoming obstacles, and growing through failure.

At its core, masculinity values merit. Success is earned, not handed out. It's built through effort, persistence, and resilience. I've coached enough men to know that when boys are told life is about ensuring everyone wins—regardless of their contributions—it sets them up for frustration and disillusionment. The masculine frame operates on clear boundaries: success or failure, victory or defeat. These aren't arbitrary or cruel distinctions; they're the crucible in which strength, character, and grit are forged. Boys grow into confident, capable men by facing challenges head-on—not by being shielded from them.

Denying boys the chance to engage in competition and experience the realities of winning and losing is a disservice. I've watched boys light up with pride after a hard-fought victory and reflect deeply after a tough loss. These moments are where growth happens. Shielding boys from failure may seem compassionate, but it strips them of the opportunity to develop resilience, adaptability, and perseverance. Comfort doesn't build character—adversity does. A boy who's never felt the sting of failure will struggle when life inevitably throws him setbacks. Rejection, challenges, and disappointment are part of life, and without the fortitude to face them, he'll find himself unprepared for the demands of relationships, careers, and personal growth.

The push for equity also sends a dangerous message: that effort doesn't matter because everyone will end up in the same place. This idea erodes the incentive to strive for excellence, sapping the very drive that fuels innovation, achievement, and progress. Boys who grow up in this environment often struggle to find motivation or purpose, having been taught to value sameness over individuality and effort. I've seen this firsthand—the lack of ambition, the apathy toward challenges, and the dissatisfaction that comes from feeling directionless. It doesn't just stifle personal growth; it weakens society by discouraging the pursuit of greatness.

Let's face it: life isn't fair, and it never will be. Outcomes are influenced by countless factors—talent, effort, timing, and even luck. Teaching boys to expect equity in results is setting them up for resentment and failure when they encounter the reality of the competitive world. Instead of focusing on outcomes, we should teach them to embrace the process of striving. The lessons learned through hard work, the pride of earning success, and the resilience built through failure are what shape strong men. These experiences aren't just beneficial; they're essential.

When masculinity is allowed to flourish, it celebrates these qualities. Boys are encouraged to take risks, push their limits, and find strength in overcoming adversity. These aren't just traits of successful individuals; they're the building blocks of strong families, communities, and societies. Effort, merit, and perseverance are the principles that propel men forward, and by instilling these values, we create a generation of men who are not only successful but also fulfilled.

The push for equity often comes with good intentions—a desire for kindness and inclusivity. But in practice, it can erase the very qualities that make life meaningful and rewarding. Boys don't need guarantees; they need challenges. They don't need sameness; they need opportunities to rise. Success is earned, and failure is not an end—it's a stepping stone to greatness. If we want boys to thrive, we must teach them to embrace the struggle, knowing it's through the climb that they'll find their strength. That's where fulfillment lies, and that's what builds men who can change the world.

Masculinity Under Siege

Feminism has undeniably made significant strides in advancing women's rights and opportunities, but I've observed how these strides often come with unintended consequences. As the push for gender equality gained momentum, a parallel narrative emerged—one that vilifies traditional masculinity. The qualities that once defined strength, responsibility, and leadership in men are now frequently labeled as oppressive or outdated. Let me be clear: this growing disdain for masculinity doesn't empower women. Instead, it creates confusion and frustration for both genders, eroding the complementary roles that once formed the foundation of strong relationships and families.

Young boys are feeling the brunt of this shift. They're constantly told to suppress their natural tendencies— assertiveness, competitiveness, and strength—and adopt traits that align with modern expectations. Messages promoting passivity and accommodation leave boys questioning their identity and place in the world. Meanwhile, young girls are encouraged to be ambitious, assertive, and career-driven. I fully support encouraging girls to realize their potential, but this shift has created an imbalance. Boys are made to feel that their inherent traits are undesirable, while girls are urged to take on qualities traditionally associated with masculinity. This reversal doesn't just confuse children; it disrupts the harmony that arises when each gender is allowed to embrace its inherent strengths.

Historically, men have taken on the role of providers and protectors—not out of a need for domination, but to create a safe and stable environment for their families. They carried the burdens of physical labor, financial responsibility, and societal leadership. Women, equally vital, contributed in complementary ways. Their nurturing, caregiving, and emotional intelligence provided the warmth and stability that turned houses into homes and children into compassionate adults. This wasn't a competition; it was a relationship. Together, these roles formed a balanced dynamic where each contribution was essential and valued.

But today's narrative seeks to erase these distinctions, promoting a one-size-fits-all approach to gender roles. Men are now expected to shoulder traditional responsibilities while being equally involved in domestic duties. On the other hand, women are encouraged to prioritize careers, often at the expense of their natural inclinations toward nurturing and emotional connection. While these shifts aim to foster equality, they frequently leave both men and women dissatisfied. Men feel undervalued for their contributions, and women experience burnout from the pressure to "do it all."

This blurring of roles undermines the unique strengths that each gender brings to relationships. Masculinity and femininity are not interchangeable; they are complementary. Men and women are biologically, emotionally, and psychologically distinct. When these differences are celebrated rather than erased, they create a balance that strengthens relationships. I've seen this balance in action, and it's undeniable: men thrive when they're allowed to lead, protect, and provide without fear of being labeled toxic. Women flourish when they can nurture, connect, and create emotional depth without being told they're limiting themselves.

Restoring this balance doesn't mean reverting to outdated or rigid roles. It's about recognizing that equality doesn't require sameness. Men and women have unique contributions, and when these contributions are honored, they create relationships rooted in mutual respect and shared purpose. True progress doesn't reject masculinity or diminish femininity—it values both. When we embrace this, we foster a society where men and women thrive together, leaning into their natural strengths and building something greater than either could achieve alone. Let's focus on celebrating the distinct qualities that make both men and women essential, and the relationships that arise when those qualities are allowed to shine.

The Importance of Cultivating Masculinity

The erosion of masculinity isn't just a cultural shift; it's a full-blown crisis with consequences that ripple through families, communities, and generations. I've seen this play out in the lives of young men, fathers, and even entire families struggling to find balance. Masculinity, when cultivated properly, isn't a threat—it's a vital force that drives stability and progress. When boys are denied the opportunity to embrace their masculine traits, they grow up uncertain of their roles and responsibilities. This isn't just about the individual; it's about the society we all live in.

Cultivating masculinity doesn't mean clinging to outdated stereotypes or rigid gender roles. It means nurturing qualities that empower boys to grow into strong, capable, and balanced men. Masculinity is more than just physical strength or assertiveness. It's a mindset rooted in responsibility, courage, and leadership. I tell parents and mentors all the time: you need to encourage boys to embrace their natural tendencies—whether through physical play, problem-solving, or leadership opportunities. These experiences help boys discover their strengths, build confidence, and learn how to navigate life's challenges.

Take physical play, for instance. It's not just about burning energy. It teaches resilience, teamwork, and the value of hard work. Problem-solving exercises go even deeper, developing critical thinking and the ability to overcome obstacles. And when boys are given leadership roles—whether in sports, school, or their peer groups—they learn accountability and the importance of guiding others with integrity. These are not just activities; they are life lessons that prepare boys to step into their roles as men.

But here's the thing: boys can't cultivate these traits in isolation. They need guidance from male role models who embody masculinity. Fathers, uncles, older brothers, and mentors play an indispensable role in this process. Boys watch how these men handle challenges, treat others, and fulfill their responsibilities. They internalize these lessons and use them to shape their own identities. When I reflect on the strongest men I've known, they didn't just teach with words—they taught through action, showing what it means to live with strength and integrity.

For boys growing up without fathers, the absence of a consistent male influence can leave a significant gap. Single mothers, while often extraordinary in their efforts, can't fully replicate the role of a father or male mentor. In these cases, it becomes essential to connect boys with positive male figures—through sports teams, community programs, or even schools. Coaches, teachers, and mentors can fill this gap, providing the guidance and discipline boys need to develop their masculine traits. Without these influences, boys often turn to media or peers for cues on masculinity, which can lead to distorted or harmful perceptions.

Media, unfortunately, doesn't do masculinity any favors. Representations are often extreme, portraying men as either hyper-aggressive brutes or completely passive pushovers. I've seen how these skewed images confuse boys, leaving them unsure of what masculinity should look like. Peer groups can also be problematic, as boys imitate behaviors driven by insecurity or bravado rather than genuine confidence. This is why intentional mentorship is so critical. Positive male role models counteract these influences, showing boys that true masculinity is about balance—strength paired with compassion, assertiveness tempered by empathy, and leadership grounded in accountability.

Cultivating masculinity isn't about rejecting femininity or diminishing the contributions of women. It's about recognizing and valuing the unique qualities that men bring to the table. Boys who grow up understanding their masculine traits become men who contribute meaningfully to their families, communities, and workplaces. They are better equipped to face adversity, take on responsibility, and build healthy relationships.

The decline of masculinity isn't inevitable—it's a challenge we can meet with intentional action and support. By fostering these traits in boys, we ensure a future where men and women thrive together, each bringing their best to the world. As a coach, a parent, or even just someone who cares about the next generation, we have a responsibility to teach boys that their masculinity is not a problem. It's a gift, one that—when nurtured—creates men who stand strong for themselves and those around them.

Balancing the Scales

While much of this chapter has focused on the challenges facing men, it's equally important to address the pressures that modern society places on women. I've seen firsthand how the cultural narrative has shifted, urging women to adopt traits traditionally associated with masculinity—competitiveness, ambition, and independence. These qualities undoubtedly have their merits, but the emphasis on them often comes at the expense of women's natural feminine strengths, such as nurturing, caregiving, and emotional intelligence. Women are often told these attributes are outdated or limiting, yet they are the very qualities that form the emotional bedrock of families, communities, and relationships.

This push for women to prioritize masculine traits creates a paradox. On the one hand, women are encouraged to excel in their careers, assert themselves in traditionally male-dominated spaces, and achieve independence. On the other hand, the value of their feminine qualities is often dismissed entirely. Many women I've spoken to feel torn between their natural inclinations and societal expectations. They feel as though they have to choose—embrace their femininity or meet the modern standard of success. Instead of celebrating the full spectrum of what women bring to the table, today's narratives often push them to focus on one end of the spectrum. The result? Burnout, dissatisfaction, and, perhaps most tragically, a loss of identity.

Encouraging women to embrace their feminine frame is not about limiting their ambitions or opportunities. Let me be clear: it's about recognizing and valuing the unique strengths they bring to the world. Feminine traits like empathy, emotional intelligence, and the ability to create deep connections are not only complementary to masculine traits but also essential for the health and stability of families and communities. When women fully embrace these qualities, they bring a richness and depth to their relationships that cannot be replicated by adopting a purely masculine approach.

Femininity is not a weakness. It's a profound strength rooted in understanding, compassion, and resilience. A woman's ability to nurture and connect emotionally serves as a critical counterbalance to the stability and protection that masculinity provides. This balance is especially evident in family dynamics. Mothers provide emotional grounding for their children, teaching lessons of empathy, communication, and care that stay with them for a lifetime. They create environments where emotional needs are met, fostering a sense of security and belonging. These contributions are invaluable, and they deserve not just recognition but respect.

Balancing the scales requires us to acknowledge a simple truth: masculine and feminine traits are both necessary for a harmonious society. Men and women are not meant to compete; they are designed to complement one another. Masculinity offers direction, strength, and stability, while femininity adds emotional depth, connection, and adaptability. When both genders embrace their natural tendencies, the contributions they make to relationships, families, and communities become greater than the sum of their parts.

For women, finding this balance also means rejecting the notion that embracing femininity somehow diminishes their worth or potential. The truth is, it's entirely possible to be ambitious and nurturing, independent and empathetic, assertive and compassionate. The false dichotomy between masculinity and femininity does a disservice to both genders. It robs men and women alike of the richness that comes from fully embracing who they are. Women who integrate their natural feminine strengths into their lives often find greater fulfillment—not because they're conforming to traditional roles but because they're honoring their authentic selves.

The way forward isn't about erasing differences. It's about redefining success to celebrate individuality and balance. When men and women lean into their unique strengths, they don't just thrive personally—they build stronger relationships, families, and communities. Balancing the scales means embracing these differences as essential and complementary forces that drive human connection and progress. This isn't about limiting anyone; it's about empowering everyone to bring their best to the table. That's how we create a society where both men and women thrive, together.

The Path Forward

To bridge the growing divide between men and women, we must abandon the false narrative that masculinity and femininity are in opposition. I've seen how this misconception sows confusion, resentment, and disconnection. The truth is simple: masculinity and femininity are not in conflict. They are complementary forces, each enriching the other in ways that create balance and harmony. Men and women were designed to work together, leveraging their unique strengths to build stronger families, communities, and relationships. But this balance can only be achieved when both genders feel encouraged—and safe—to embrace their natural roles without fear of judgment, ridicule, or rejection.

The modern narrative too often pits masculinity against femininity, as if one's success comes at the other's expense. Let me tell you, this divisive thinking benefits no one. Instead of collaboration, it breeds competition and misunderstanding. The reality is far more hopeful: masculinity and femininity are two halves of a whole. Together, they form the foundation for stability, connection, and progress. Men and women were never meant to compete for dominance; they were meant to collaborate. Each gender brings strengths to the table that, when combined, create something far greater than either could achieve alone.

The solution to this divide begins with education. From an early age, boys and girls need to be taught to understand and value their inherent strengths. Boys should feel empowered to embrace their natural assertiveness, competitiveness, and resilience while learning to temper these traits with empathy and responsibility. Similarly, girls should be supported in developing their emotional intelligence, compassion, and adaptability while also being encouraged to pursue their ambitions with confidence. When education emphasizes the value of both masculinity and femininity, we foster mutual respect and understanding. Boys and girls who grow up appreciating these qualities become adults who can collaborate effectively in their relationships and communities.

Parenting is another critical piece of the puzzle. Parents have the greatest influence over how children perceive gender roles and relationships. Fathers must model masculinity, showing strength, accountability, and kindness in their actions. Mothers, on the other hand, should embrace and exemplify the power of femininity, demonstrating how nurturing and emotional depth strengthen families and communities. In single-parent households, it's vital to connect children with positive role models of the opposite gender—through extended family, community programs, or mentors. When children see both masculine and feminine traits valued in action, they grow up with the confidence and respect needed to navigate life's complexities.

Relationships themselves must also evolve. Relationships flourish when both men and women feel valued, respected, and understood. Men need the space to lead, protect, and provide without fear of being labeled oppressive or outdated. Women need the freedom to nurture, connect, and create emotional depth without being told they're limiting themselves. These roles are not rigid or prescriptive; they're flexible frameworks that allow each individual to bring their best to the relationship. When men and women embrace their natural tendencies, they create dynamic relationships that strengthen both individuals and the union as a whole.

Reclaiming the balance between masculinity and femininity isn't just about individual relationships; it's about building a stronger, more cohesive society. Families rooted in this balance are more stable, raising children who understand their own strengths and respect those of others. Communities thrive when men and women collaborate, each bringing complementary qualities to shared goals. A society that values both frames is not only more resilient but also more innovative and connected.

The path forward requires courage. It demands a willingness to challenge the entrenched narratives that have divided us for too long. It requires honesty—about how modern culture has eroded mutual respect and understanding between genders—and intentional action to rebuild that respect. Whether through education, parenting, or relationships, we must create space where both men and women can thrive in their natural strengths.

This journey won't be easy. Change rarely is. But it is necessary. By embracing the complementary nature of masculinity and femininity, we can build a future where men and women work together, creating stronger families, healthier relationships, and a more unified society. The effort we invest today will shape a better tomorrow—not just for us, but for generations to come. Let's begin the work of bridging this divide. The future depends on it.

Chapter 3:
Feminism's False Promises and the Truth About Gender Dynamics

Let's get one thing straight: we've been sold a lie. The narrative that women can "have it all" has been repeated so often that it feels like an undeniable truth. On the surface, it sounds like the ultimate form of enablement—a message of liberation and endless opportunity. But when you strip away the shiny veneer and examine the foundation, you'll find cracks that have left countless women and men feeling frustrated, confused, and disillusioned. It's not just a harmless myth; it's a deeply flawed promise that ignores the realities of life, energy, and priorities. Feminism—particularly in its modern form—has shifted from advocating for equality to fostering resentment and imposing unrealistic expectations. It's no longer a movement aimed at creating harmony; it has become one that fuels division.

I've observed this transformation with a growing sense of concern. Women are told they can excel in every area—career, relationships, motherhood—without making trade-offs. They're told that depending on a man, or even collaborating with one, diminishes their worth. They're told that embracing their feminine nature—the very essence of who they are—is somehow a betrayal of their potential. Let me tell you something: this isn't liberation. It's a setup. It's a carefully packaged trap that promises fulfillment while delivering exhaustion and emptiness. Life doesn't work that way. When you try to pour yourself fully into every aspect of life without prioritizing or making sacrifices, you eventually run out of energy, time, and joy.

This trap doesn't just affect women. It affects men, too. Modern feminism often sells the idea that men are unnecessary or even harmful. Women are encouraged to view men not as allies or people but as obstacles to their success. Meanwhile, men are left feeling alienated, as if their natural instincts to lead, provide, and protect are no longer valued. This isn't progress—it's chaos. Men and women are designed to complement each other's strengths, but when resentment and unrealistic expectations enter the equation, that collaboration breaks down.

I believe it's critical to address this head-on because the stakes are too high to ignore. I've seen the toll this takes on relationships, careers, and personal well-being. Women chasing the illusion of "having it all" often find themselves burned out, unfulfilled, and questioning why they still feel empty despite their achievements. Men, on the other hand, feel marginalized, unsure of their roles, and hesitant to step into the leadership and protection they were designed for.

Let me be clear: this isn't about blaming feminism as a whole. There was a time when the movement sought meaningful progress, advocating for women's access to education, voting rights, and career opportunities. Those were necessary steps forward. But modern feminism has taken a turn—a turn that prioritizes resentment over collaboration, division over connection. If we continue down this path, the fractures in our personal and societal relationships will only deepen. It's time to break free from the illusion and start building a new framework that honors the strengths of both men and women.

First, let's dismantle the myth of unequal rights. Feminists often claim that women live under systemic oppression, but the reality tells a very different story. Women today enjoy every legal right men do—and in some cases, they hold advantages that men do not. The problem isn't the absence of equality; it's the failure to recognize where disparities exist and how they affect both genders. Let me walk you through some of the most glaring examples.

Let's start with reproductive rights. This is an area where the disparity is not just apparent—it's staggering. Women have absolute authority over whether to bring a child into the world. The decision to continue or terminate a pregnancy rests entirely in their hands. Meanwhile, the man involved has no legal input once conception occurs. If a woman decides to have the child, the man is legally bound to provide financial support, regardless of whether he's emotionally, mentally, or financially prepared for fatherhood. He doesn't get to opt out. This isn't just about fairness—it's about accountability. While I believe every man should step up and take responsibility for his actions, I also believe he should have some level of recourse in situations where he had no say in the outcome. This imbalance isn't just overlooked; it's actively ignored by a society that claims to champion equality.

Now, let's turn to the professional world. Feminists frequently argue that women are paid less than men for the same work, perpetuating the idea of a "wage gap." But when you step back and apply a little logic, this claim doesn't hold up. If businesses could hire women to do the same job as men for less money, why wouldn't they hire only women? It would be a simple and effective way to maximize profits. The reality is that the so-called wage gap isn't the result of systemic discrimination—it's rooted in the choices men and women make about their careers, industries, and work hours.

Women, on average, gravitate toward careers in fields that pay less, such as education, healthcare, and social work. These fields are valuable, but they don't generate the same revenue or demand the same risks as industries like finance, technology, or construction—industries where men are more likely to work. Men are also more likely to take on dangerous jobs, work longer hours, and pursue careers in highly competitive, high-stress environments. These decisions directly impact earning potential. It's not a matter of sexism; it's a matter of preferences and priorities.

The narrative of a systemic wage gap creates unnecessary tension and distracts from the real issues at hand. Instead of focusing on fabricated disparities, we should be having honest conversations about the choices individuals make and the trade-offs those choices entail. Equality isn't about identical outcomes; it's about providing equal opportunities and respecting the different paths people choose to take. Anything else is just noise.

Let's talk about sports, a clear example of how economic reality determines outcomes. Professional female athletes often voice concerns about earning significantly less than their male counterparts. On the surface, this disparity might seem unfair, but when you dig into the economics of the situation, the answer becomes clear. Revenue drives pay—plain and simple. Men's sports leagues, such as the NBA, generate billions of dollars in profits through ticket sales, sponsorships, merchandise, and television rights. These profits create the financial foundation that supports high salaries for male athletes. In contrast, leagues like the WNBA have struggled for decades to turn a profit. Despite years of effort, the WNBA remains subsidized by the NBA, the very organization its advocates sometimes criticize.

This isn't about gender discrimination—it's about basic economics. Revenue, not gender, determines what athletes earn. If a league or organization generates significant income, its athletes reap the benefits. If it doesn't, there's simply no money to distribute. Let's be honest: demanding "equality" in pay without creating equal value isn't fairness—it's entitlement. Imagine asking a business to pay its employees exorbitant salaries while losing money every year. No one would call that a sound business model; it's financial suicide. The same principles apply to sports. When you strip away the emotions, the truth becomes unavoidable: athletes are paid in proportion to the revenue they help generate.

The real problem isn't just misinformation about pay disparities—it's the emotional fuel behind the conversation. Feminism, particularly in its modern form, thrives on presenting women as perpetual victims of an unfair system. Men, by extension, are cast as oppressors who benefit at women's expense. This narrative isn't just flawed—it's damaging. It alienates both genders and perpetuates a sense of division that prevents real progress.

Men are left feeling villainized for simply existing. Even when they've done nothing wrong, the societal conversation often frames them as part of the problem. Meanwhile, women are burdened with an impossible standard: they're told to be strong, independent, and successful while juggling the innate human desire for connection, family, and purpose. Feminism claims to liberate women, but in many ways, it has done the opposite. It has created an environment where women are expected to excel in every area without acknowledgment of the inherent trade-offs.

This is where I believe we need to step back and apply a dose of logic. Success—whether in sports, business, or personal life—is about value creation. Men's sports leagues thrive because they capture massive audiences and drive substantial profits. Female athletes, like anyone in any profession, should focus on building that same level of value if they want comparable rewards. It's not sexism; it's economics. The narrative that blames men or systemic inequality for these differences only fuels resentment and obscures the actual issue: the need to create something people are willing to support at scale.

When we replace emotional rhetoric with clear thinking, we can have honest conversations about these dynamics. Feminism shouldn't focus on tearing others down—it should focus on lifting women up through real strategies that enable them to succeed based on merit and value. Anything less is a distraction from what truly matters.

Here's where the irony deepens: modern feminism claims to fight for women's freedom, yet in practice, it often undermines the very choices it claims to protect. Think about it—freedom implies the ability to make decisions that align with your personal values and desires. But when those decisions don't fit the mold prescribed by feminist ideology, they're often met with criticism or outright disdain. One glaring example is how women who choose to focus on raising a family are frequently dismissed as "wasting their potential." Instead of celebrating their choice, they're labeled as regressive or even complicit in perpetuating outdated gender roles. How can a movement that claims to empower women justify judging them for following their instincts and prioritizing their families?

Let me be clear: true enablement isn't about steering women toward one predefined version of success. It's about recognizing that every woman has her own unique priorities and allowing her to pursue them without fear of judgment. For some, that path might involve climbing the corporate ladder, breaking barriers in their field, and becoming leaders in the professional world. For others, it's about nurturing a family, raising children, and creating a home filled with love and stability. And for many, it's a combination of the two—

a dynamic mix of professional ambition and personal fulfillment. The key is that the choice should belong to the individual, not dictated by societal expectations or ideological pressure.

I've seen this conflict play out countless times. A woman chooses to step back from her career to focus on raising her children, and instead of receiving support or understanding, she faces criticism. Comments like, "Why would you give up your career?" or "You're setting women back" are all too common. This kind of rhetoric isn't just unkind—it's hypocritical. If feminism is truly about freedom, then why does it stigmatize women who exercise that freedom in ways that differ from the prescribed norm? The truth is, this isn't liberation—it's control. It replaces one form of societal pressure with another, leaving women to navigate a new set of expectations that are just as restrictive.

True liberation embraces the full spectrum of choices available to women. It acknowledges that no single path fits everyone. It also recognizes that fulfillment isn't measured by external standards but by internal alignment with one's values. A woman who finds joy and purpose in raising her children is no less empowered than one who thrives in the boardroom. The same goes for women who juggle both roles. What matters is that the choice is made freely and authentically, without coercion or condemnation.

We need to challenge this ironic contradiction head-on. If we're serious about empowering women, we must support their choices—whether they align with modern feminist ideals or not. Liberation means removing barriers, not building new ones. It means celebrating diversity in paths and priorities rather than enforcing a narrow definition of success. Let's stop judging women for doing what feels right for them and start honoring their freedom to live life on their terms.

Let's address the elephant in the room: relationships. If we're being honest, modern feminism has profoundly disrupted how men and women relate to one another. What used to be an intricate dance of mutual respect and understanding has devolved into a battleground of mistrust and division. Modern dating is a prime example. Women are often encouraged to view men as adversaries—people who will inevitably take advantage, manipulate, or fail to meet their expectations. On the flip side, men, sensing this undercurrent of suspicion, retreat into apathy or defensiveness. Rather than fostering connection, these dynamics breed isolation, resentment, and, ultimately, dysfunction.

Let me tell you, this isn't progress—it's chaos. Healthy relationships aren't built on suspicion or power struggles. They thrive when both parties acknowledge, respect, and even celebrate their differences. Men and women were designed to complement one another. The strengths of one naturally offset the weaknesses of the other, creating a synergy that enhances their shared experience. But this synergy becomes impossible when one side is trying to dominate or dismiss the other. Unfortunately, modern feminism often prioritizes the narrative of female liberation at the expense of men's contributions, leaving both genders feeling undervalued and misunderstood.

Now, let's get to the root of this problem: the so-called patriarchy. Feminists love to shout about this vague, all-encompassing concept as if it's the ultimate cause of every difficulty women face. But let's unpack this idea for a moment. The patriarchy, as it's commonly described, is little more than a scapegoat for life's challenges. It's a convenient target for blame when things go wrong. Women are encouraged to see the system as inherently oppressive rather than examining how their own decisions, circumstances, or efforts might have contributed to their setbacks.

This deflection is not only misguided—it's harmful. When you teach someone to always blame external forces for their problems, you rob them of the opportunity to grow. Accountability is the cornerstone of maturity, and without it, personal development becomes impossible. Let me share something I've learned from years of observing human behavior: growth begins when you take ownership of your choices, no matter how difficult or uncomfortable that might be. Without accountability, we're trapped in a cycle of blaming others and repeating the same mistakes.

Jack Nicholson's famous line about how his character rates a woman sums it up perfectly: "I think of a man, and I take away reason and accountability." As harsh as it sounds, this observation highlights a glaring issue within modern feminist rhetoric. By encouraging women to shift responsibility onto an abstract concept like the patriarchy, feminism undermines their ability to assess their own actions and make meaningful changes. This isn't enablement—it's a disservice.

The truth is, life is full of challenges, and not all of them are caused by systemic oppression. Some are simply the result of choices, circumstances, or chance. Enablement doesn't come from blaming the system; it comes from understanding what you can control, taking responsibility for your actions, and making adjustments where necessary. Relationships, like personal growth, thrive on this principle. Men and women both need to step into accountability—not as adversaries, but as collaborators seeking mutual respect and understanding. Until we reclaim this fundamental truth, our connections will continue to suffer under the weight of mistrust and blame.

Now, let me make something abundantly clear: I'm not here to bash women. In fact, it's the opposite. I believe women are extraordinary—capable, intelligent, and absolutely vital to the fabric of our world. They bring unique strengths, perspectives, and skills that enrich every area of life, from families to workplaces to communities. But here's the thing: the path to true fulfillment for women—or for anyone, really—isn't paved with resentment, denial, or unrealistic expectations. It's found in understanding who we are, respecting the differences that make us unique, and collaborating in ways that make the whole stronger than its parts. Men and women were never designed to stand in opposition. They're meant to complement each other, to work together in harmony, not engage in some ideological tug-of-war over who holds more value or power.

This brings us back to the concept of "having it all," a mantra that has been sold as a symbol of liberation but, in reality, often leads to frustration and disillusionment. Life, whether we like it or not, is a series of trade-offs. Every decision we make has an opportunity cost. Pursuing one goal almost always means sacrificing another. That's not oppression—it's just the way things work. Let me explain.

Imagine a woman who dedicates herself to building a high-powered career. She puts in the long hours, makes the sacrifices, and achieves the professional success she's been striving for. That's incredible, but it often comes at a cost. For many, that cost might be delaying or even forgoing starting a family. Relationships and parenthood require time, energy, and emotional investment—resources that are finite. On the other hand, a woman who chooses to prioritize her family might find that her career advancement slows down, or she decides to step back entirely for a period. Again, this isn't a failure or a limitation—it's simply the reality of making intentional choices.

What feminism often fails to acknowledge is that these trade-offs are not punishments or evidence of inequality. They're universal truths of life. Men face similar dilemmas, though the societal pressure points may look different. The problem arises when society tells women that they should be able to excel at everything simultaneously without compromise. That kind of messaging sets them up for inevitable disappointment when they realize they can't stretch their time, energy, and focus infinitely.

I've seen this play out too many times. Women who bought into the idea that they could "have it all" find themselves burned out, juggling too many roles, and wondering why they still feel unfulfilled. It's because fulfillment doesn't come from trying to do everything at once—it comes from doing what aligns with your values and priorities. True enablement isn't about pretending trade-offs don't exist; it's about making choices that resonate with who you are and what truly matters to you.

The conversation we need to have isn't about pushing women to do more or discouraging them from pursuing their ambitions. It's about being honest about the costs and encouraging everyone to make intentional, informed decisions about their lives. Fulfillment comes not from external achievements alone but from internal alignment. When men and women recognize this truth, they can stop competing with unrealistic expectations and start living lives of purpose and authenticity.

What about men in all of this? It's impossible to have an honest conversation about modern gender dynamics without addressing the impact on men. Modern feminism has left many men disoriented, unsure of their place in a rapidly shifting cultural landscape. They've been told to embrace sensitivity while simultaneously suppressing their natural strength. They're encouraged to step back to make room for women to rise. But when they comply, when they adopt a softer or more passive demeanor, they're often met with criticism. Suddenly, they're labeled weak, uninspiring, or unmanly. This double bind creates a sense of confusion and resentment—an emotional limbo where men feel they can't win no matter what they do.

Let me be clear: asking men to embrace sensitivity and empathy isn't inherently wrong. In fact, these are valuable traits that can deepen connections and build understanding. But the problem arises when this call for sensitivity comes at the expense of men's natural instincts to lead, protect, and provide. These instincts are not flaws to be erased—they're core to who men are. Suppressing them doesn't help anyone; it creates men who feel lost and disconnected from their sense of purpose.

I've seen this confusion firsthand. Men who once carried themselves with confidence and a clear sense of direction now second-guess their every move. They hesitate to step into leadership roles, unsure if they'll be criticized for being too assertive. They hold back in relationships, afraid that their protective instincts will be labeled as controlling. This erosion of masculine identity isn't just a personal crisis for these men—it has ripple effects on their relationships, families, and communities. When men lose touch with their natural roles, everyone suffers.

Here's what I believe: men need to rediscover and embrace their natural roles as leaders, protectors, and providers—not to dominate, but to uplift. Leadership, when done with integrity and empathy, isn't about controlling others; it's about creating stability and direction. Protection isn't about infantilizing women; it's about offering support and security when needed. Provision isn't limited to financial resources—it's about bringing value, vision, and strength to the table. These roles, far from being outdated or oppressive, are essential to thriving connections between men and women.

Similarly, women must reclaim their feminine essence as nurturers and connectors. This isn't about restricting women to traditional roles; it's about recognizing and celebrating the strengths that are naturally aligned with their instincts. Nurturing doesn't mean weakness—it means fostering growth, empathy, and connection. Women are uniquely equipped to bring emotional depth and adaptability to relationships, qualities that complement men's strength and stability. When women embrace these traits without feeling diminished by them, they step into their full power.

These roles aren't restrictive—they're complementary. Men and women were designed to bring different strengths to the table, and it's in embracing these differences that we find balance. The narrative that pits men and women against each other is a destructive one. Thriving relationships aren't about competition; they're about collaboration, respect, and mutual understanding. When both genders lean into their natural roles, they create a dynamic that lifts both parties, allowing each to shine in their unique way.

For men, the journey back to their natural roles starts with rejecting the idea that masculinity is toxic or outdated. True masculinity, grounded in accountability, empathy, and strength, is a force for good. For women, reclaiming their feminine essence means letting go of the fear that nurturing and connection somehow make them less than. Together, these shifts can rebuild the foundation for relationships, families, and communities that thrive—not through sameness but through the celebration of complementary strengths.

Let's shift the focus to solutions. How do we navigate this cultural quagmire where gender roles have been blurred, misunderstood, or outright dismissed? The answer lies in rejecting the false dichotomy that modern feminism has created. Feminism often suggests that in order for women to rise, men must step back—that progress for one gender requires diminishing the other. This is a flawed and divisive premise. True progress doesn't come from tearing anyone down; it comes from recognizing and embracing the inherent value that each gender brings to the table. Men and women are not identical, and they shouldn't strive to be. Instead, they should lean into their unique strengths, recognizing how these differences can complement one another to create a dynamic that fosters growth, trust, and purpose.

Let's talk about what this means for men. It starts with reclaiming your confidence and sense of purpose. The narrative that masculinity is inherently toxic has done tremendous damage, leaving many men feeling uncertain about their roles, hesitant to assert themselves, and unsure of their value. Let me tell you something that needs to be said: there is nothing wrong with being a man. Masculinity, when rooted in integrity, accountability, and empathy, is a powerful force for good. It provides stability, protection, and direction—qualities that are not just beneficial but essential in relationships, families, and society at large.

Men, it's time to stop apologizing for your masculinity. Embrace it. Stand tall. Be assertive, take responsibility, and lead with strength and compassion. Leadership doesn't mean domination—it means stepping into the role of someone who provides clarity and guidance, someone who others can trust to make tough decisions with wisdom and fairness. This isn't about proving your worth to anyone else; it's about recognizing it within yourself.

I've seen too many men shrink themselves in an attempt to fit the mold of what society now expects. They suppress their instincts to lead or protect because they're afraid of being labeled as overbearing or out of touch. But here's the truth: women don't need men who shrink to make them feel empowered. That's not liberation—it's a façade. What women truly need are men who stand firm, who embrace their role as protectors and providers, and who bring stability, direction, and support to the table.

This isn't about overshadowing women; it's about complementing them. A man's strength doesn't undermine a woman's power—it enhances it. When a man leads with integrity and confidence, he creates an environment where a woman can fully step into her strengths, whether that's in nurturing, connecting, or pursuing her own ambitions. Together, this dynamic creates a synergy that allows people to thrive.

The solution isn't for men to retreat or for women to dominate—it's for both to step into their natural roles with clarity and purpose. Men, reclaim your space. Be strong, but also be empathetic. Be assertive, but also be kind. True masculinity isn't about overpowering others; it's about creating a foundation where everyone around you can grow and flourish. Stop listening to the noise that tells you to be less. Instead, focus on being the best version of yourself— strong, confident, and unapologetically masculine.

For women, the message is equally clear: you don't have to prove your worth by rejecting your femininity.

Feminism has often framed liberation as a rejection of traditional roles, encouraging women to downplay their nurturing qualities in favor of ambition. But let me tell you something important—being ambitious doesn't mean you have to abandon your nurturing instincts. And being nurturing doesn't mean you have to sacrifice your ambitions. The two are not mutually exclusive. In fact, you are at your most powerful when you embrace the full spectrum of who you are, combining your drive with your ability to connect, care, and foster growth in others.

Feminine traits—empathy, adaptability, and emotional intelligence—are not weaknesses. They are strengths, and society desperately needs them. Women have a unique capacity to build bridges, create harmony, and inspire collaboration. These qualities are not in conflict with ambition; they enhance it. A woman who embraces her femininity alongside her professional or personal aspirations is a force to be reckoned with. She isn't confined to a single identity; she thrives in multiple dimensions because she honors every part of herself.

Here's where modern feminism has failed women: it has sold them a narrative of scarcity. It suggests that men and women are locked in competition, fighting for a finite pool of resources, opportunities, and success. This couldn't be further from the truth. Men and women are not adversaries, nor are they interchangeable. They were designed to bring unique strengths to the table, and when those strengths are combined, the result is far greater than what either could achieve alone.

Think of it like this: men often excel in bringing structure, strength, and vision to any endeavor. These traits create the foundation and the framework necessary for progress. Women, on the other hand, bring depth, connection, and adaptability. They have an unparalleled ability to read emotional undercurrents, adapt to changing circumstances, and inspire collaboration. These qualities don't compete with masculine traits—they complement them, creating a dynamic that amplifies success, whether in relationships, families, or professional environments.

Collaboration between men and women isn't just beneficial—it's essential. When men and women lean into their natural strengths, they create something extraordinary. Men provide the strength to hold the structure together, while women infuse it with life and meaning. Together, these qualities create a synergy that enhances every aspect of life. It's not about one gender overshadowing the other; it's about working together to create something greater.

The feminist movement, in its earlier forms, sought to empower women by breaking down barriers and opening doors. That was a necessary and noble mission. But somewhere along the way, the message shifted. Instead of focusing on collaboration, it began promoting competition, teaching women to see men as obstacles to their success. This perspective only breeds resentment and alienation, making it harder for both men and women to thrive.

True enablement isn't about competing with men or proving that you can do everything they can. It's about recognizing your unique strengths, embracing them, and working alongside men to build something meaningful. When women step into their full power—unapologetically feminine and ambitious—they inspire not just themselves but everyone around them. The world doesn't need women who suppress their instincts to fit a mold. It needs women who boldly embrace every aspect of who they are, knowing that their contribution is invaluable.

The truth is, men and women don't thrive in isolation or opposition. They thrive in collaboration when each gender brings its best to the table. By rejecting the false narrative of scarcity and embracing the unique strengths of both men and women, we can create a society that's more dynamic, innovative, and connected. That's the real power of leaning into who we are—together.

The path forward requires something that has been sorely lacking in the conversation about gender dynamics: courage and honesty. These two qualities are essential if we are to break free from the narratives that have divided us and begin building something better. It starts with acknowledging the damage that has been done—not as a way to assign blame, but as a way to understand where we've gone wrong. Divisive ideologies, for all their lofty promises, have left deep scars on how men and women view themselves and each other. It's time to stop perpetuating these harmful narratives and instead choose a path that fosters collaboration, respect, and mutual growth.

For men, the challenge is stepping back into their natural roles without fear. Society has done a thorough job of convincing men that their strength, leadership, and protective instincts are oppressive relics of the past. But that's a lie, and it's time to let it go. Men, you have a vital role to play, and reclaiming that role isn't about dominating—it's about uplifting. Lead with integrity. Protect with kindness. Provide with confidence. Your contributions are not just necessary; they're invaluable. Stepping into these roles unapologetically is not an act of oppression—it's an act of service, one that benefits everyone around you.

For women, the journey forward is equally transformative. It's about embracing your unique strengths without succumbing to the external pressures that demand you abandon them. The world doesn't need women who feel compelled to prove they can outmatch men in every arena. It needs women who are confident in their feminine essence and who understand that their nurturing, connecting, and empathetic qualities are strengths—not weaknesses. This isn't about rejecting ambition; it's about integrating it with the full spectrum of who you are. There is extraordinary power in being both driven and deeply in touch with your instincts, and when women fully step into that space, they inspire everyone around them.

Let me make one thing clear: this isn't about reversing progress—it's about redefining it. Progress isn't a zero-sum game where one gender wins only if the other loses. True progress honors the strengths of both men and women, recognizing that we are at our best when we work together, not against each other. It's about moving forward in a way that allows everyone to thrive.

In conclusion, the lie of "having it all" has taken a toll. For many women, it has resulted in exhaustion, disillusionment, and the sense that they are somehow falling short despite their best efforts. For men, it has led to marginalization and the loss of a clear sense of purpose. But here's the good news: we don't have to stay stuck in this place. There is hope. By rejecting the false narratives that divide us and embracing the strengths that define us, we can create a new understanding of what it means to be men and women in today's world.

This isn't just about surviving—it's about thriving. It's about creating a future where both genders are allowed to step into their roles without fear or resentment. Together, men and women can build stronger relationships, healthier families, and a more cohesive society. But it starts with courage—the courage to question the stories we've been told and the honesty to embrace the truths we've overlooked. The path forward isn't easy, but it's worth it. Because when we move together, honoring our differences and celebrating our strengths, we don't just survive—we thrive. Together

Chapter 4:
The Dangers of Red Pill Ideology and the Role of Leadership in Relationships

We live in a time where ideologies are shaping relationships in ways that undermine their very foundation. Feminism has already done enough damage, but there's another growing movement that threatens to wreck relationships: the Red Pill ideology. I've seen it all — the podcasts, the YouTube videos, the forums where men spew hatred and resentment, not just towards women but towards their own ability to relate to them. It's a movement that promises truth, but what it really offers is a distorted view of men, women, and relationships.

Let me be clear: I'm not here to sugarcoat things. Red Pill rhetoric has misled men into thinking that women are the enemy. The term "AWALT" (All Women Are Like That) has become a battle cry for men who've bought into this toxic ideology. The movement tells men that women are manipulative, self-centered, and incapable of loving them the way they want to be loved. It feeds into a sense of betrayal and hopelessness. This isn't just misguided; it's dangerous.

The Red Pill movement has gained significant traction in recent years, but make no mistake: it is a dangerous ideology that poisons the minds of men. At its core, it presents itself as the "truth" about women, claiming that women are inherently manipulative, self-serving, and incapable of fulfilling a man's needs. According to this movement, society has deceived men into thinking that women are equal companions, but in reality, they are only out for their own selfish interests. This concept is rooted in one of the most toxic and misguided worldviews I've seen in modern times. Let me be clear, men: this is not enlightenment — it's a distortion of reality.

What the Red Pill ideology does is sell men a deeply cynical view of women and relationships. It teaches men to distrust women and to see them as adversaries instead of potential spouses. Men who adopt this mindset start viewing every woman through a lens of suspicion and fear. They generalize women as manipulative and deceitful, assuming that any woman they encounter is just like the ones they hear about in Red Pill forums or watch in YouTube videos. The tragic consequence of this mindset is a rift between men and women, a growing divide built on distrust, misunderstanding, and miscommunication.

Understand this: relationships, whether they are romantic, familial, or professional, are founded on trust. If you strip trust away, there's nothing left. It's the bedrock of every meaningful connection. When you let yourself fall into the trap of seeing women as the enemy, you lay the foundation for relationships that will inevitably crumble. You build walls instead of bridges. You close yourself off from the possibility of a real, genuine connection. And when that happens, all you're left with is isolation, bitterness, and resentment.

The Red Pill movement often uses the term "AWALT" (All Women Are Like That), perpetuating the idea that all women are manipulative, untrustworthy, and ultimately unworthy of a man's trust. The ideology also encourages men to "go their own way" — to avoid relationships altogether in favor of self-preservation. This is the essence of MGTOW (Men Going Their Own Way). The core message here is simple: women are a threat, so men should focus solely on themselves and avoid any form of intimate connection with women. Let me be blunt: this is not a conscious escape from the complexities of relationships; it's a cowardly retreat from life itself. It's a decision to isolate, to shut out one of the most fulfilling and enriching parts of life: connection with another human being.

MGTOW and Red Pill thinking make men blind to one of the most powerful forces in life: the power of connection. True relationships — relationships where both parties contribute and care for one another — bring growth, fulfillment, and joy. They challenge us, help us become better people, and provide us with experiences that would be impossible to achieve alone. Retreating from relationships doesn't shield you from harm; it shields you from opportunity. When you run from real human connection, all you do is build up walls around yourself. You prevent yourself from living a full, rich life. It's not strength; it's stagnation. And I can't think of anything more dangerous than that.

The Red Pill movement misrepresents women in the most harmful way. It turns them into one-dimensional villains. According to this ideology, women are all deceitful and manipulative — as if those traits are universal to every woman. But the truth is far more complex than that. Women, like men, are multifaceted human beings. They have strengths and weaknesses, just like everyone else. Some women may act in ways that are harmful or manipulative, but that doesn't mean every woman fits that description. Just as it would be foolish to stereotype men based on the actions of a few, it's equally misguided to stereotype women. Every woman is not the same, just as every man is not the same. And when you fail to recognize the individuality of each person you encounter, you strip yourself of the opportunity to form meaningful, enriching relationships.

I've seen the pain and frustration that lead some men to latch onto these ideologies. The hurt of feeling betrayed or misunderstood in relationships can drive men to seek solace in these distorted views. I get it. But I'm here to tell you this as clearly as possible: the road to happiness, fulfillment, and success in relationships is not paved with distrust, isolation, and resentment. It's paved with understanding, communication, and mutual respect. The solution to your pain is not to shut yourself off from women or to label them as adversaries. The solution is to engage with women — and men, for that matter — with an open mind, a level head, and a deep respect for who they are as individuals.

Men who cling to the Red Pill doctrine only create lives filled with bitterness and emptiness. They close themselves off from the possibility of experiencing love, companionship, and genuine connection. They cut themselves off from one of life's greatest gifts — true emotional intimacy. While there are nuggets of truth to red pill theory - which is nothing more than someone's take on gender dynamics you have to search for them and apply them in such a way that your relationship or future relationship can flourish. Most of these ideas are built on fear, distrust, and a warped understanding of human nature. The real truth lies in connection, mutual respect, and respect for the natural roles that men and women each bring to relationships. These aren't just buzzwords. They are essential truths that lead to fulfilling relationships. The key to a successful relationship is not about trying to "beat" the other person; it's about understanding them and learning to work together to achieve something greater than either of you could achieve alone. That's the foundation of true happiness and connection. Let go of the toxic rhetoric. Embrace real connection. Let go of past misconceptions and embrace the future with open eyes.

MGTOW, or "Men Going Their Own Way," is a dangerous philosophy that has gained traction in recent years, and it's important to understand exactly why it is so detrimental. At its core, the movement encourages men to avoid relationships with women altogether. The premise? Women are a threat to men's well-being. MGTOW followers argue that women are manipulative, self-serving, and ultimately damaging to a man's life. They claim that relationships with women are dangerous and that men are better off focusing on themselves and avoiding any romantic entanglement with women. But let me be clear: this mindset is not a solution — it's a self-imposed prison. It's a retreat from life itself.

When men adopt MGTOW, they cut themselves off from something essential to their humanity: connection. Men were never designed to live in isolation. Our lives are shaped, defined, and enriched by the relationships we have with others. Real, deep, and meaningful relationships are where life happens. Life is not meant to be a solitary pursuit, with no one to share the highs, the lows, or even the mundane moments. A man's life should not be lived solely for his own benefit. It should be lived alongside someone who supports him, challenges him, and walks with him through life's inevitable ups and downs. That's what true success looks like. It's not just about personal achievements; it's about sharing those achievements with someone who cares, who adds value, and who helps you grow into the best version of yourself.

The tragedy of MGTOW is that it's not just a rejection of women; it's a rejection of intimacy, connection, and personal growth. The movement encourages men to shut themselves off from one of the most fulfilling aspects of life. Sure, a man can focus solely on his career, personal goals, and financial success, but at what cost? What's the point of achieving personal milestones if you don't have someone to share them with? Life without someone to celebrate with, someone to talk to, and someone to lean on becomes hollow. MGTOW turns men into islands, isolated from the very connections that enrich our lives and help us grow. And isolation is never the answer.

Men are not meant to live in a vacuum. Men and women were designed to complement each other. We learn from each other. We challenge each other. We help each other grow. The power of relationships lies in this dynamic — the exchange of ideas, experiences, support, and love that helps both people evolve. When a man isolates himself from this dynamic, he denies himself the opportunity to grow. He may think that he's protecting himself, but in reality, he's stunting his own personal development. The isolation that MGTOW promotes leads to stagnation, not growth.

The foundation of MGTOW is fear. It's rooted in the fear that women will take advantage of men, that men will lose control in relationships, and that their lives will be disrupted by romantic involvement. I get it. Men have been hurt, betrayed, and disappointed by relationships in the past. It's painful. But here's the reality: fear is not a path to strength. Fear only limits growth. When a man steps into his role as a leader, when he is grounded in his masculinity and knows who he is, relationships no longer need to be a source of fear. Leadership is not about control; it's about taking responsibility and making decisions. Leadership is about providing direction, not domination. A man should lead, not dominate, and when he leads, there is no fear of losing control. Leadership gives clarity, stability, and vision.

MGTOW, however, suggests that men should avoid relationships altogether to maintain control over their lives. But in reality, what men are avoiding is growth.

Relationships challenge us. They push us to grow, to learn, to become more than we were. Relationships provide opportunities to develop as individuals in ways that solitary living cannot. If a man avoids relationships because he fears losing control, he's missing out on the chance to step up, take responsibility, and lead a life that is richer, more fulfilling, and full of opportunities for growth.

I urge you to rethink this philosophy, especially if you've found yourself entangled in MGTOW thinking. Yes, personal growth and self-improvement are essential. Focus on building yourself into the best version of who you can be, but recognize this: human beings were made for connection. Relationships are not a threat. They are an opportunity for growth, love, and fulfillment. Do not let fear dictate your life's path. Relationships should not be seen as risks to avoid but as opportunities to thrive. A connection with another person offers challenges, yes, but it also offers tremendous rewards. The right relationship can help you become the man you are meant to be, providing support, challenge, and love in ways that no solitary existence ever will.

Let's be clear: it's easier to stay in your comfort zone. It's easier to isolate yourself from the risk of vulnerability and potential hurt. But the growth you're seeking will only come through engagement with others — through real, honest connections. A solitary existence may seem safe, but it's also deeply limiting. MGTOW promotes an illusion of freedom, but in reality, it's nothing more than an escape from the deeper, more fulfilling aspects of life.

So stop hiding. Stop retreating. Life, true life, is lived with others. Relationships offer you the chance to build something greater than yourself — to learn, to grow, and to become a stronger, better man. When you open yourself up to the possibilities of connection, you embrace the true power of relationships. Don't let fear close the door on that. Step into your life and into relationships with confidence, purpose, and the knowledge that it is through connection — not isolation — that you will truly thrive.

Leadership in a relationship is not optional. It is absolutely essential. Too many men today have abdicated their responsibility as leaders in their relationships, and the consequences are clear. Whether it's a conscious choice or an unconscious slip, this failure to lead creates confusion and frustration and ultimately sets the stage for the relationship's collapse. A relationship without leadership is like a ship without a captain — it's directionless, purposeless, and it has no steady hand to guide it through life's inevitable storms.

A man must step into his role as a leader with complete confidence. Leadership is not about being domineering or controlling; it's about taking responsibility. It's about understanding that the buck stops with you. Leadership in a relationship is about providing clarity, direction, and stability. It's about being the one who sets the course when things get uncertain, who makes the tough calls, and who remains steady when chaos looms. A man who refuses to lead leaves his significant other adrift. And that, my friends, is a recipe for disaster.

You might think leadership means controlling every aspect of your significant other's life, but that's not what I'm talking about. Leadership is not about micromanaging your significant other's thoughts, actions, or decisions. Leadership is about setting the tone for the relationship. It's about demonstrating reliability, decisiveness, and accountability. When a man leads, he offers his significant other a sense of security. He creates an environment where his woman can feel safe, supported, and able to embrace her own feminine energy. Leadership in a relationship isn't about dominating; it's about showing strength in your actions and decisions, which then allows your significant other to soften and thrive in her role as a nurturer and supporter.

Let me tell you something that is non-negotiable: if you are not leading your relationship, you are setting it up for failure. A relationship without direction is doomed to stagnation. It will struggle to move forward. Women are drawn to strong, decisive men who know who they are and what they want. That's the kind of man who can take charge when needed but also step back and let his better half shine when the time is right. A man who is uncertain about his path, or worse, who lets his significant other take the reins, will quickly create a toxic, unsteady dynamic that will crumble under pressure.

When a man leads, he doesn't just give direction to the relationship; he allows his other half to step into her own role. A woman thrives when she can embrace her femininity, when she doesn't feel like she has to bear the weight of leadership herself. A man who leads allows his significant other to step into her role as a supporter, as someone who nurtures and cares for the emotional aspects of the relationship. Both companions are able to operate from a place of respect and mutual understanding, where the roles are clear, and both feel fulfilled.

Leadership in a relationship means being reliable and responsible. It means that when things get tough, your significant other knows that she can count on you to be the steady hand that guides the ship. It's not about being perfect; it's about being consistent. You must be someone who is dependable, who shows up every day, and who handles the challenges life throws at you with confidence and clarity. A woman doesn't want a man who is constantly wavering, who can't make a decision, or who doesn't know what he wants. That's not leadership; that's uncertainty. Women are looking for men who lead with certainty, who take charge when necessary, and who have the vision to move the relationship forward.

When a man refuses to take on his leadership role, he denies his significant other the security she needs. Relationships need direction, and without it, they falter. If you are hesitant about leading, if you leave decisions to your significant other or allow her to take charge in areas where you should be stepping up, the relationship loses its equilibrium. A woman needs to feel safe in her relationship. She needs to know that her man is the one who will take charge when needed, who will lead through uncertainty, and who will be the steady hand that keeps them moving forward.

The truth is simple: men who don't lead their relationships will fail to cultivate the kind of deep, meaningful connection that both companions need. A woman wants security — emotional, physical, and mental. She wants to know that her man is the one who provides that security by being decisive, being clear, and taking responsibility for both his own life and the relationship. A woman who feels she needs to lead the relationship herself will eventually grow frustrated, resentful, and fatigued. This is not her role. It's the man's role to take the lead, and when he does, both thrive.

A key aspect of leadership is being able to recognize that you are not perfect. You don't need to have all the answers all the time, but you do need to be the one who is willing to take responsibility for decisions, to course-correct when things go wrong, and to step up when life gets challenging. Real leadership in a relationship doesn't come from a place of control; it comes from a place of accountability. You are accountable for the direction of the relationship, for the emotional well-being of your significant other, and for the quality of the connection you share.

Women are drawn to strong men, but not the type who lead with an iron fist or try to control their significant other's every move. Leadership is about strength and vulnerability in equal measure. It's about knowing when to be firm and when to soften, when to take charge, and when to listen. It's about guiding with humility, taking responsibility, and leading by example.

If you are not stepping into your leadership role, you are neglecting the most critical part of the relationship. Relationships do not thrive in chaos or uncertainty. They thrive in an environment where both people know their roles in the relationship, where the man leads with purpose and strength, and where the woman feels safe and supported. Leadership means making decisions, setting the tone, and carrying the responsibility. It means not letting your significant other carry the emotional load of the relationship and instead being the anchor they can rely on. When you do this, the relationship will find its true potential.

So, let me be clear: relationships need leadership. If you don't take the reins, your relationship will flounder. If you don't lead with clarity, confidence, and purpose, you will create a vacuum that no one can fill. Leadership is what allows people to flourish, to step into their roles fully, and to create something much stronger together than they could individually. When you take responsibility and lead with integrity, the relationship will thrive. Step up and lead because if you don't, you're setting yourself up for failure. Period.

In every relationship, the dynamics between masculinity and femininity are the driving forces that determine its success or failure. These dynamics aren't simply social constructs or arbitrary roles; they are deeply embedded in our biology, our psychology, and our emotional needs. Men and women are fundamentally different in their approaches to life, love, and relationships. These differences are not weaknesses — they are strengths. However, the problem today is that these differences are often misunderstood and mishandled. Both men and women are encouraged to step outside of their natural roles, which only leads to confusion, frustration, and conflict.

Let me make this as clear as possible: men are naturally inclined to lead. Women are naturally inclined to nurture and support. These roles are not interchangeable, and when they are forced to be, the relationship suffers. The masculine role of a man is to lead, to protect, and to provide. These are not optional; they are intrinsic to a man's role in any successful relationship. When a man steps fully into his masculine role, he creates the space for his significant other to step into her feminine role — to nurture, support, and connect emotionally. This isn't just an idea; it's the foundation of a healthy relationship. This dynamic creates equilibrium, an unspoken harmony that allows both people to thrive. Relationships are like a dance — it's a give and take, where each person contributes their own unique strengths. When the roles are clearly defined and embraced, the relationship becomes greater than the sum of its parts.

When a man fails to step into his masculine role, he forces his significant other into a situation where she must take on masculine responsibilities — and this is where many relationships break down. Women do not want to lead their relationships. This is not in their nature. Women want to feel supported, protected, and led. They don't want to have to make every decision. They want to feel secure in the strength of their significant other. When a man refuses to lead, a woman is left with no choice but to step into the masculine role herself. She must take on the responsibilities that are rightfully his. This dynamic disrupts the natural flow of the relationship, and frustration inevitably begins to build.

Women are nurturers. It's not just a role; it's a calling. But when they're forced into roles that require them to lead, protect, and provide in the same way that a man should, they become emotionally drained, resentful, and disconnected. I've seen it countless times: men who fail to lead their relationships force their spouses into roles they were never meant to play. This leads to resentment — not because women dislike their significant other, but because they are being asked to be something they were never meant to be in the relationship.

Men, your job here is simple: step into your role. Be the leader. Don't avoid it, don't procrastinate. Embrace your masculinity and all the strength that comes with it. Step into your role as the leader, protector, and provider. Lead with confidence, lead with clarity, and lead with integrity. You were made for this. Women, your role is just as important. Embrace your femininity. Allow yourself to soften, to nurture, to support. Recognize that when both people step fully into their natural roles, the relationship becomes stronger, more harmonious, and ultimately more fulfilling.

I cannot stress this enough: when both individuals embrace their natural roles, the relationship thrives. When men take charge of their masculine responsibilities, they create a space where women can step into their feminine roles with grace, softness, and emotional depth. Women are able to embrace their nurturing nature without the burden of leadership. They don't have to fight for control. They don't have to be the ones making all the decisions. They can lean into their significant other's strength, which allows them to fully embrace their own role as the emotional center of the relationship.

This dynamic is what makes relationships thrive. It's what keeps them strong, even in the face of adversity. When a man leads, and a woman supports him, the relationship doesn't just survive; it flourishes. There's a synergy that happens when both people embrace their natural roles. The man becomes the steady foundation, and the woman brings emotional richness and connection. The relationship becomes a well-oiled machine, both individuals contribute equally but in different ways.

So, men, here's the truth: your leadership is crucial. If you don't lead, if you don't take charge, you're making it impossible for your woman to step into her feminine role. You're forcing her into a masculine frame that will drain her. You are denying both of you the opportunity to experience the depth, connection, and harmony that comes with embracing your natural roles.

And women, understand this: your femininity is your strength. You are not meant to lead. You are meant to support, nurture, to emotionally connect with your significant other. Embrace that. When you allow your man to step into his role as the leader, you create a relationship that thrives, a relationship where both people feel respected, supported, and fulfilled.

When both parties step into their respective roles, the relationship becomes a dance, a harmonious exchange where each person's strengths are magnified. A man leads with strength, clarity, and purpose. A woman nurtures with love, empathy, and emotional depth. This synergy creates an equilibrium that fosters mutual respect and fulfillment.

The problem today is that these roles have been blurred, and too many people are stepping outside their natural roles. Men are avoiding their role as leaders, and women are stepping into roles they were never meant to fill. This leads to confusion, frustration, and disconnection. The solution is simple: step into your natural role. Embrace who you are meant to be in the relationship. Men, lead with confidence and integrity. Women, embrace your nurturing role with grace and softness. When both of you do this, the relationship becomes what it's meant to be — strong, fulfilling, and unshakable.

Stepping into your masculine role as a man is not just an option — it's non-negotiable. If you want your relationship to thrive, you must lead. Period. There is no room for passivity, no space for indecision. If you want to be a great companion, a great lover, and a great leader in your relationship, the first place to start is with yourself. You must lead your own life. You must know who you are, where you're going, and what your vision is. Only when you're grounded in your own masculinity can you offer the stability your significant other needs to truly thrive.

This isn't about being "macho" or dominating your significant other. That's not leadership — that's insecurity wrapped in aggression. True masculinity is about being present, being decisive, and taking responsibility. It's about standing firm when the storms of life roll in and providing clarity when your significant other feels uncertain. Leadership is about being able to take the reins when necessary and knowing when to step back, allow your significant other to contribute, and give her space to shine. It's knowing when to act and when to listen. It's about creating a vision for the future and guiding the relationship toward that vision with strength and purpose.

The truth is harsh but necessary: if you're not leading in your relationship, you are failing. There's no way around it. Your woman wants to feel secure. She wants to feel like she's with a man who has direction, who has purpose, and who is unwavering in his commitment to both himself and the relationship. She wants to know she can trust you, not just with her heart, but with the future — that you have what it takes to handle the challenges life throws at you both. If you fail to step into your role as the leader, you deprive her of the stability she needs. Without that stability, the relationship will always feel like it's in a state of limbo.

When you step up as the leader, you give your woman the freedom to embrace her feminine role. She can soften, nurture, and support you in ways that strengthen the entire relationship. This dynamic is a synergy that can't be replaced. You provide the security she craves, and she provides the emotional depth and support that fuels the connection. When people step into their respective roles, the relationship flourishes. A woman who feels secure in her man's leadership is free to step into her role as the emotional anchor. She can give more of herself because she trusts the stability you bring to the relationship.

But if you're not stepping up, you're not just failing your significant other — you're failing yourself. Women are drawn to strong, decisive men. Not men who are wishy-washy or uncertain, but men who know who they are and where they are going. Men who are grounded in their masculinity have clarity in their decisions, confidence in their actions, and unwavering strength when times get tough. The moment you fail to lead, you lose your significant other's trust. She may not say it directly, but she will start to question whether you're the one she can rely on when life gets hard. And let's be real — if she doesn't feel like she can rely on you, then what is the point of the relationship?

Leadership is about direction. It's about taking responsibility for your life and the relationship you're building. It's not about being perfect; it's about being reliable. Your woman needs a man who will be there, who will act with integrity, and who will make the tough calls when needed. That's what leadership is — it's stepping up consistently to guide the relationship, to make decisions, and to provide the security and stability that your significant other needs.

So, let's get real: Man up. Step into your role as the leader you're meant to be. Lead with confidence, clarity, and strength. Embrace your masculinity fully and unapologetically. This is your role in the relationship, and when you step into it, you'll see the transformation. Your relationship will no longer be stuck in confusion, uncertainty, or frustration. It will flourish under your guidance. You will be respected, trusted, and admired for the strength you bring to the relationship. And your woman will feel safe, supported, and secure.

Leadership is the backbone of any successful relationship. Anything less than that is a disservice — to yourself and your better half. So stop waiting for the perfect moment. Stop hesitating. Step into your masculine frame, take the reins of your life and your relationship, and lead with clarity and purpose. That is how you create success in relationships and, more importantly, how you create a life that you're proud to live.

Chapter 5:
A Blueprint for Men

Men often find themselves trapped in the myth that sacrificing their own needs will somehow lead to happiness in their relationships. This misconception has been perpetuated for generations, wrapped in sayings like "happy wife, happy life," as though a man's worth in a relationship is measured solely by his ability to please his significant other. However, this path of self-sacrifice rarely works. In fact, it sets men up for failure on multiple levels. It doesn't just compromise their sense of self; it undermines the very foundation of mutual respect that is essential in any meaningful relationship.

When a man consistently sacrifices his own needs, he inadvertently signals that his priorities and feelings are less important. Over time, this creates a dynamic where his significant other may begin to lose respect for him. Respect is not something that can be demanded or negotiated; it is earned through consistent actions that demonstrate strength, integrity, and self-worth. A man who continuously prioritizes someone else's happiness at the expense of his own risks becoming resentful and disconnected from his true self. This disconnection is felt not only by the man but also by the significant other, who may interpret this lack of self-respect as a lack of leadership and confidence.

Let me explain why this dynamic often leads to irreparable damage in relationships. Respect is the cornerstone of connection. Without it, love cannot thrive, trust cannot deepen, and desire cannot be sustained. When a man loses respect for himself, he sets the stage for his significant other to follow suit. It's not about being domineering or self-centered; it's about maintaining an equilibrium where both individuals feel valued and respected. Sacrificing your needs might seem noble in the short term, but it erodes the foundation of mutual respect over time. Eventually, the relationship becomes a shadow of what it could have been, leaving both parties unfulfilled.

Understanding this dynamic is the first step toward reclaiming your role as a man who leads with strength, confidence, and purpose. Leadership in a relationship doesn't mean exerting control; it means setting an example. It means demonstrating through your actions that your needs and boundaries matter just as much as those of your significant other. When you hold yourself to a high standard, you inspire those around you to do the same. This doesn't just benefit you; it creates a dynamic where the relationship can flourish, built on a foundation of mutual respect and admiration.

So, let's dismantle the myth of self-sacrifice. True fulfillment in a relationship comes from authenticity, not martyrdom. It's about showing up as your best self, not as a watered-down version of who you think you need to be to keep someone else happy. When you lead with confidence and purpose, you create an environment where respect can thrive, and with it, a relationship that stands the test of time.

Respect is the cornerstone of any meaningful connection. It underpins every aspect of a healthy relationship, serving as the foundation upon which love, trust, and desire are built. Without respect, even the strongest bonds will erode over time. Love may falter, trust may waver, and the spark of desire may fade. This isn't conjecture—it's a reality I have observed a pattern in the lives of men and women struggling to maintain their relationships.

A woman's respect for a man doesn't come from empty gestures or performative acts of chivalry. It stems from the man's ability to uphold his own standards, to act with consistency, and to demonstrate through his actions that he values himself. When a man operates with integrity, doing what he says he will do and standing firm in his principles, he earns the respect of those around him, including his significant other. This respect isn't something you can demand; it's something you cultivate through your character and actions.

Let me be clear about one thing: parroting clichés like "happy wife, happy life" is a surefire way to lose respect. This mindset reduces a man to a passive participant in his own life, someone who prioritizes appeasement over authenticity. While women may outwardly appreciate the sentiment, deep down, they cannot respect a man who sacrifices his self-worth in an attempt to maintain harmony. This isn't leadership; it's capitulation, and it sets the stage for resentment on both sides.

Respect is earned through action. It's about showing up consistently and handling your responsibilities with competence and confidence. When a man fails to prioritize his own needs and values, he sends a message that he doesn't consider himself worthy of respect. If you don't respect yourself, how can you expect someone else to? This lack of self-respect is palpable, and it erodes the dynamics of the relationship.

Women are naturally drawn to strength, not in the sense of physical dominance, but in the strength of character. They admire a man who knows who he is and what he stands for. A man who operates with clarity and purpose exudes a confidence that is magnetic. Conversely, a man who constantly seeks to please at the expense of his own integrity loses that sense of strength, becoming someone who is difficult to respect.

To earn and maintain respect, you must first respect yourself. This means holding yourself to a high standard, honoring your commitments, and living in alignment with your values. It means standing firm when it's easier to compromise and speaking the truth even when it's uncomfortable. Women respect men who lead with conviction and authenticity, not those who mold themselves to fit someone else's expectations.

Respect is not a one-time achievement; it's a continual process. It requires vigilance, self-awareness, and a commitment to personal growth. When you consistently demonstrate that you value yourself, you create an environment where mutual respect can flourish. This, in turn, strengthens the relationship, allowing both individuals to thrive. If you want to build a meaningful connection, start by understanding that respect is the foundation—and it begins with you.

Here's the truth: a woman's happiness isn't your responsibility. It's hers. Happiness is an internal state, not something you can gift or negotiate. She may carry unresolved issues from her past, attachment disorders, or dissatisfaction with her own life, and none of this is yours to fix. These struggles may shape her outlook and reactions, but they do not define your role in the relationship. Your job is not to bend over backward to make her happy. Instead, it's to build a life and character that commands respect and admiration. When you focus on your own growth and purpose, you create a dynamic where true connection can thrive.

Let me emphasize this: you cannot solve someone else's internal battles. Whether it's childhood trauma, insecurities, or personal dissatisfaction, these are challenges that only she can confront and resolve. Your well-meaning attempts to fix these issues will likely backfire, leaving you drained and her unfulfilled. Happiness is a personal journey, and each individual must walk their own path to find it. No matter how much you care or how hard you try, you cannot force someone to be happy if they are not willing to do the work themselves.

Instead of expending energy trying to fill a void that isn't yours to fill, focus on becoming the best version of yourself. This isn't about ignoring her needs or being selfish; it's about understanding that your value in the relationship comes from your strength, confidence, and purpose. When you prioritize your own growth, you set an example that inspires and uplifts those around you. A man who knows his worth and lives in alignment with his values creates an environment where respect and admiration can flourish.

If she cannot find happiness within herself, no amount of effort from you will change that. This doesn't mean you're indifferent to her struggles; it means you recognize the limits of your influence. Supporting her doesn't mean fixing her. It means being present, listening without judgment, and encouraging her to take ownership of her journey. True connection isn't about solving each other's problems; it's about growing together while respecting each other's individuality.

Remember, a strong relationship is built on two whole individuals coming together, not one person trying to complete the other. By focusing on your own growth, you not only become a better man but also create the conditions for a healthier and more fulfilling connection. Prioritize your purpose, uphold your values, and let go of the misguided belief that you are responsible for someone else's happiness. When you embrace this mindset, you allow both yourself and your significant other to thrive in the relationship and beyond.

When a relationship falters, it's an opportunity to reflect and recalibrate. Rather than succumbing to blame or bitterness, take stock of what went wrong and what role you played in the dynamic. Growth begins with accountability. Recognize the decisions, actions, or behaviors that may have contributed to the breakdown. This isn't about self-criticism; it's about self-awareness. Learning from your experiences is the first step toward building stronger connections in the future.

Let me be clear: moving forward doesn't mean rushing into another relationship. Healing takes time, and genuine growth requires deliberate effort. Instead of seeking validation or comfort from someone new, focus on improving yourself. Address the wounds from the past, rebuild your confidence, and refine your understanding of what you truly want in a relationship. This period of self-improvement isn't just beneficial; it's essential. Without it, you risk repeating the same patterns and encountering the same frustrations.

Not all women are the same, and not all relationships will mirror the past. The idea that all women share the same tendencies or issues is not only unfair but also limiting. You will meet someone who respects, admires, and complements your strengths. However, attracting such a connection requires you to become the kind of man who naturally inspires those qualities. Respect, admiration, and genuine connection are not things you can demand; they are reflections of the person you are.

To prepare for the relationship you desire, you must first become the man worthy of it. This means addressing your shortcomings, honing your strengths, and living with purpose. A man who is grounded, confident, and self-aware creates an aura of respect and admiration that draws others to him. Conversely, a man who carries unresolved baggage or lacks direction will struggle to form meaningful connections.

Healing and growth are not passive processes. They demand intention and effort. Read, learn, and engage in activities that challenge and uplift you. Surround yourself with people who inspire you to be better. Take care of your physical and mental health, as these are foundational to your overall well-being. When you invest in yourself, you not only enhance your own life but also create the conditions for a healthier and more fulfilling relationship in the future.

Moving forward doesn't mean forgetting the past; it means learning from it. Each experience, whether positive or painful, holds lessons that can shape your future. Embrace these lessons, and let them guide you toward becoming the best version of yourself. The right connection will come when you are ready, and when it does, you will be prepared to nurture it with the wisdom and strength you've gained.

You can't negotiate for love, respect, or desire. These are not commodities to be bartered or begged for; they are earned through the strength of your character and the consistency of your actions. Love rooted in genuine connection, respect forged through integrity, and desire sparked by authenticity are powerful forces. They cannot be coerced or contrived. They emerge naturally when you show up as the man you aspire to be.

Once you have earned these, understand this truth: you cannot take them for granted. Respect and admiration are not static. They demand ongoing effort and vigilance. Relationships thrive on consistent growth and mutual appreciation. When you become complacent, you risk losing the very elements that make the connection strong and enduring.

Maintaining respect requires self-awareness and a commitment to self-improvement. It's not enough to earn admiration at the start of a relationship; you must continue to demonstrate the qualities that inspired it. This involves setting up and upholding clear standards and boundaries. Without these, the relationship will falter, drifting into confusion and dissatisfaction. Standards are not about control; they are about clarity. They define what you expect, what you value, and what you are willing to give in return.

Clarity is power. When you are clear about your values, your goals, and your expectations, you bring certainty to the relationship. This clarity is not only attractive but also stabilizing. It allows both you and your significant other to navigate the connection with confidence and purpose. Without it, misunderstandings and unmet expectations breed resentment.

To cultivate a relationship built on love, respect, and desire, define what you want with precision. Reflect on what matters most to you in a connection. Consider the qualities you value in yourself and in a significant other. Be honest about your non-negotiables and communicate them with conviction. When you lead with clarity, you attract a connection that aligns with your vision.

Earning love, respect, and desire is not a one-time accomplishment. It is a continuous journey of growth, self-awareness, and purposeful action. Show up with intention, and you will create a dynamic where these elements flourish, not as fleeting moments but as enduring foundations of a meaningful relationship.

There's nothing more captivating than a woman fully in her feminine energy. This state is not about superficial traits or societal stereotypes; it's about a deep, intrinsic essence that radiates confidence, grace, and authenticity. When a woman feels truly safe and secure in a relationship, she accesses a part of herself that is both alluring and inspiring. Her feminine energy is not something that can be forced or manufactured; it emerges naturally when she feels respected, cherished, and emotionally secure.

This energy has a magnetic quality that words often fail to describe. It's a presence that fills the room, an aura that commands attention without demanding it. When a woman embraces her feminine energy, she exudes a warmth and openness that draws people in. This isn't about playing a role or fulfilling societal expectations; it's about being fully present and authentic in her own skin. Her femininity is her strength, not a weakness, and it has the power to elevate not only herself but also those around her.

For men, this dynamic is transformative. When you encounter a woman who is fully in her feminine energy, it awakens something primal and profound within you. It draws out your masculinity in a way that feels natural and powerful. This isn't about dominance or control; it's about equilibrium. Her openness invites your strength, and your strength creates a space where her vulnerability can thrive. Together, this interplay creates a connection that is both powerful and irresistible.

However, this dynamic doesn't happen by chance. It requires you to show up consistently as the man she respects and desires. Respect is earned through your actions, your words, and your presence. It's about being dependable, confident, and authentic. Desire is sparked not by manipulation or pretense but by the genuine connection you foster through your character and actions. When you embody these qualities, you create an environment where her feminine energy can flourish.

Let me emphasize this: the safety and security she feels are paramount. This doesn't mean shielding her from every challenge or difficulty; it means being a steady presence she can rely on. Your ability to handle your own life with confidence and purpose allows her to relax into her own authentic self. When she doesn't have to question your intentions or your reliability, she can fully embrace her femininity without fear or hesitation.

The interplay between masculine and feminine energy is a dance, not a contest. It's about complementing each other, not competing. When both energies are allowed to exist in their fullest forms, the connection becomes something extraordinary. Your masculinity doesn't overshadow her femininity; it enhances it. Her femininity doesn't diminish your masculinity; it amplifies it. Together, you create a dynamic that is not only balanced but also deeply fulfilling.

It's important to note that feminine energy is not static. It ebbs and flows, influenced by emotions, circumstances, and the dynamics of the relationship. As a man, your role is not to control or direct this energy but to create an environment where it can thrive. This means being attentive, empathetic, and self-aware. It means understanding that her emotional expression is not a weakness but a strength. By honoring her emotions and supporting her growth, you allow the connection to deepen and evolve.

The magnetic power of feminine energy is a gift, but it's a gift that requires care and appreciation. When you take the time to nurture this dynamic, you unlock a level of connection that goes beyond the superficial. It's not just about chemistry or attraction; it's about a profound understanding and appreciation of each other's essence. Her femininity inspires your masculinity, and your masculinity empowers her femininity. Together, you create a relationship that is both powerful and harmonious.

It's time to face an uncomfortable truth: many of you aren't doing enough. This isn't about just making her happy—it's about something deeper, something more enduring: respect. I've seen it time and time again. Men can survive without love. But respect? That's a different game. Men crave respect more than anything, and when that respect fades, so does the foundation of the relationship. The moment it slips away, the relationship starts to unravel. If you think your love for her will keep things together, you're missing the point. Respect is the core that holds everything intact. Without it, you're just two people going through the motions.

Respect is earned. It's not a given. It's not automatic, and it's certainly not something that you can demand. You can't shout your way into respect, and you can't expect it because you've been in a relationship for a while. Respect is built over time, through actions, consistency, and honesty. If you're wondering why things are falling apart, why she's pulling away, or why the tension is growing, I'll tell you: It's because you haven't been delivering.

When you fail to show up consistently, when you fail to meet the expectations you've set, respect erodes. Let me explain. Women don't just want promises. They want results. They want action. The moment you say one thing and do another, the cracks begin to form. This is a reality check: women can see through your facade. They can sense when you're projecting a false image, trying to be something you're not, or trying to sell them an illusion. And when that facade is cracked, when the truth comes through, their respect for you vanishes.

It's not just about big gestures or grand promises. It's about the everyday consistency, the reliability, and the accountability you show. It's the small actions that build the foundation of respect. Do what you say you'll do, when you say you'll do it. That's where it starts. Be a man of your word. If you can't deliver, don't promise. You may think she's not paying attention, but trust me, she is. Women are far more attuned to these inconsistencies than you think. And once they see that you can't deliver, once they see that you're not as dependable as you claim, the respect slips away.

But the issue goes deeper than just fulfilling promises. The problem arises when you don't have a solid sense of self. In my experience, Men, uncertain of their own identity, create an image of themselves that they think will impress her. They try to be something they're not, and while it may work for a while, it never lasts. You can't sustain a false image. The real you will always emerge eventually. And when that happens, the respect she once had for you will disappear, because she'll feel like she's been deceived. She won't respect the man who pretends to be something he's not. It's not about being perfect; it's about being real. Authenticity is the backbone of respect.

Furthermore, understand that respect isn't a one-way street. It's reciprocal. You want her respect? Show her respect. It's that simple. If you're not treating her as an equal participant in the relationship, if you're not valuing her opinion, if you're not listening to her, you're setting yourself up for failure. A relationship is built on mutual respect, and that doesn't just apply to her respecting you—it applies to you respecting her as well. It's a dynamic, an exchange, an understanding. It's about giving as much as you expect to receive.

But let me be clear: respect is not about submission. It's not about you bending over backward to please her or letting her walk all over you. That's not respect, that's weakness. And women don't respect weakness. They may tolerate it for a while, but they won't stick around if that's all you have to offer. Women respect strength—emotional strength, mental strength, and moral strength. You need to show that you can stand firm, make decisions, and take responsibility. Women want a man who leads, a man who takes charge of his own life and isn't afraid to make tough calls when necessary.

It's also crucial to understand that respect is not about being dominant, controlling, or inflexible. Being a man of respect means you can show up confidently in your life, in your work, and in your relationship. It means taking responsibility for your actions, making decisions based on your values, and standing by those decisions, even when things get tough. And when you make mistakes, as we all do, owning up to them and learning from them. That's where real respect is built—through accountability.

I've witnessed countless men lose respect from women because they think it's enough to show up and go through the motions. It's not. If you want her to respect you,

you have to show up in every aspect of your life—personal, professional, and relational. Don't just be present—be present with purpose. Let your actions reflect who you are and what you stand for. The moment you stop doing this, the moment you take her and the relationship for granted, is the moment you start losing her respect.

So, what can you do about it? Start with yourself. Look at who you are and what you're bringing to the relationship. Are you being the man you expect her to respect? Are you delivering on your promises, living authentically, and showing respect in return? If not, it's time to make a change. It starts with being a man of integrity, a man who leads by example, and a man who can handle both success and failure with grace.

If you want respect, you have to earn it. And to do that, you must show up, consistently. Hold yourself accountable. Lead by example. Be real. Show strength and vulnerability where necessary, but always be someone she can rely on. When you do that, respect will follow. When you don't, the consequences are clear: it slips away, and the relationship starts to crumble. Respect is the foundation of everything. Start building yours, now.

The foundation of being a man is simple: do what you say you will do. No excuses. No shortcuts. If you commit to something, follow through. You don't get a pass just because the task seems small or inconvenient. The real measure of your character comes down to how you handle the little things. These aren't trivial tasks; they're opportunities to show that you care, that you're capable, and that you can be relied upon.

Handle your responsibilities with integrity. Whether it's tightening a loose door handle or fixing an aging ceiling fan, it's not about the task itself. It's about your ability to act when needed. It's about proving you're someone who gets things done, who follows through, and who doesn't leave loose ends hanging. These are the details that create a sense of trust. These are the moments that build your reputation as a man who can be counted on.

Don't dismiss the small tasks because they seem insignificant. When you neglect them, you're sending a message. It's the same as saying, "I'm too busy" or "That's not important." But in reality, these little things matter. They matter to her. They matter because they show that you take pride in your environment, in the space you share, and in the people you care about. When you take care of these things, you show that you're dependable, that you can handle the demands of life, and that you're not afraid of responsibility.

When you handle your shit, you create an environment where she feels safe, valued, and secure. From experience, I can tell you: a woman is much more likely to respect you when she knows she can count on you to take care of business. It's not about grand gestures. It's about consistency. The little actions, the day-to-day reliability, are what make a woman feel truly supported. When she knows you'll take care of the house, the car, the bills, and the tasks, big and small, she feels that she's not carrying the weight alone. She feels that she can lean on you—and that's when the trust builds.

Respect isn't just a feeling you get; it's something you create. And you create it by doing what you say you'll do. Being reliable, responsible, and taking charge of your life creates an atmosphere of respect and security. You don't need to be perfect, but you do need to be accountable. Show her that you're someone who follows through, who doesn't make excuses, and who takes pride in the commitments you've made.

This is what it means to be a man. Not just a man who talks a good game, but a man who backs it up with action. Your words mean nothing without your actions to support them. If you say you're going to do something, do it. Don't put it off. Don't leave it half-finished. When you're a man of your word, you build trust. And trust is the foundation of everything. Without it, nothing else matters. When you follow through, you show that you're capable, reliable, and that you care enough to make sure things get done.

This isn't about being perfect. It's about being consistent. When you make the effort to fix the small things, you demonstrate that you're paying attention to the details of life and to the people in your world. You create a space where she can feel safe, valued, and secure, because she knows you're a man who takes responsibility. This is the foundation of respect, and it's the foundation of being a man.

Your physical appearance and health matter more than you think. Women aren't drawn to the idea of a "dad bod" as much as they're drawn to confidence and vitality. Let's face it—taking care of your body isn't just about looking good; it's about showing discipline, respect for yourself, and a commitment to leading by example. When you're in shape, you don't just feel better—you project an aura of authority and confidence that others instinctively respect.

Think about it: when you step onto a plane and see a fit, sharp-looking pilot, you immediately feel a sense of reassurance, right? There's an unspoken trust there. The same principle applies in relationships. A man who takes care of himself inspires trust and admiration. Why? Because it signals that you take your own well-being seriously. You're a man who values himself enough to put in the work—physically, mentally, and emotionally.

Now, consider this: if you're out of shape, it's time to make a change. No more excuses. Hit the gym, refine your style, sharpen your hygiene. These may seem like small actions, but their impact is significant. When you start investing in yourself, you change the way the world perceives you—and, more importantly, how you perceive yourself. A man who takes pride in his appearance and health doesn't just look good; he feels good. He exudes a sense of confidence that naturally attracts respect and admiration from others.

Taking care of yourself is a sign of self-respect. It shows that you're not content with just existing. You're actively striving to be the best version of yourself, and that kind of mindset is powerful. Women are naturally drawn to men who have their shit together, who show that they're capable, committed, and responsible. When you make the effort to stay in shape, to dress well, and to maintain good hygiene, you create an impression that lasts.

This isn't about vanity. It's about projecting a version of yourself that commands respect. It's about putting in the effort to ensure you're presenting your best self to the world. Your physical appearance is one of the first things people notice about you, and while it's not everything, it definitely plays a role in how you're perceived. A fit, well-groomed man exudes a level of control and confidence that others can't help but notice.

I'll tell you this: it's easy to let things slide, to get comfortable, to let your physical health deteriorate. But doing so only sends the message that you don't care. You don't care about your body, your health, or your image. And that lack of self-respect will affect every area of your life, including your relationships. The truth is, taking care of yourself is one of the most powerful ways to show that you respect not only yourself but those around you as well.

So, get off your ass and make the change. Start hitting the gym, eat better, and take pride in your appearance. Get out of your comfort zone. The results won't be immediate, but they will be lasting. When you put in the work, you'll not only transform your body, but you'll transform your mind and your energy. This shift in how you feel about yourself will radiate outward, attracting people who respect you and who are inspired by the man you're becoming.

Remember: the way you look on the outside reflects the way you feel on the inside. A man who takes care of himself is a man who has something to offer—something that others can't help but admire. So, take care of your body, refine your style, and sharpen your hygiene. These small but significant actions will elevate your self-worth, change how the world perceives you, and empower you to lead by example in every aspect of your life.

As a man, you set the tone for those around you. It's not just about your actions—your energy, your attitude, and your approach to life will influence everyone in your circle, especially those closest to you. If you're disciplined, focused, and driven, your significant other and your family will naturally follow suit. They'll pick up on your habits, your work ethic, and your mindset. Your behavior becomes the blueprint for how they navigate their own lives.

Conversely, if you're lazy, unmotivated, and neglectful, don't be surprised when those qualities ripple through your household. Your actions will speak louder than any words. If you're not setting the standard, don't expect others to rise to a level that you're not willing to maintain yourself. The energy you bring to the relationship determines the energy that flows through your home. If you're complacent, don't be shocked when others are too.

Leadership isn't about control. It's about inspiring others through your actions. True leadership isn't found in barking orders or demanding respect. It's about showing up every day as the best version of yourself—being the type of person you want those around you to become. People watch you, consciously or unconsciously, and they'll pick up on your habits. This means that the energy you bring into the room can either lift everyone up or drag them down.

Think about it: leadership doesn't require a title. You don't need to be the boss to be a leader. The most effective leaders lead by example. It's the small things that matter— the discipline to get out of bed early, the focus to complete tasks without procrastination, the drive to keep pushing even when things get tough. These are the traits that others notice. When you embody these qualities, others will gravitate toward them. They'll see how you operate, how you handle challenges, and how you keep pushing forward despite obstacles. That's the kind of leadership that inspires respect.

You want your family to be motivated? Be motivated yourself. Want your significant other to be driven? Be driven yourself. Want your children to be disciplined? Show them what discipline looks like. Your actions will always speak louder than your words. If you lead by example, you don't need to force anything. People will follow your lead because they will see the results of your mindset. They'll see your progress, and they'll want to mirror that.

When you make the effort to set a high standard for yourself, you're not just raising your own expectations—you're raising the bar for those around you. This isn't about perfection; it's about consistency. It's about showing that you can be relied upon, that you're someone who operates with intention and focus. When you do this, it's not just you who benefits—it's everyone in your circle. You become a catalyst for positive change.

Let me be clear: leading by example isn't always easy. There will be days when you don't feel like pushing through. There will be times when you'll want to slack off. But true leaders don't let their feelings dictate their actions. They show up, even when it's hard. They keep moving forward, even when motivation is low. They inspire others through their perseverance and their commitment to the work at hand.

You are the standard. You set the bar. So, raise it. When you lead by example, you don't just change your life—you change the lives of everyone around you. You inspire them to rise higher, to strive for more, and to become the best versions of themselves. The influence you have is far greater than you realize, and it all starts with you.

Respect, love, and admiration aren't static—they must be nurtured and cultivated every single day. A relationship isn't a trophy you win and place on a shelf to admire; it's a living entity that requires constant care and attention. It evolves. It grows. It needs both men and women to be actively engaged, committed, and constantly working to build something stronger. You can't afford to become complacent. If you want respect and admiration, you must be willing to earn it consistently, not just once in a while.

Define your standards and uphold your boundaries. Know exactly what you will tolerate and what you won't. Establish a clear sense of who you are and what you stand for, and don't waver from that. When you do this, you not only create clarity in your own life, but you also create an environment where your significant other knows what to expect and what's expected of them. You both get to thrive when you're both showing up as the best versions of yourselves. This takes effort, consistency, and a firm commitment to your principles.

The relationship you have, whether it's romantic, familial, or professional, is a reflection of the man you are. The future you want begins with the decisions you make today. If you want a future filled with respect, love, and admiration, you need to be the man who consistently earns it. And that doesn't happen by chance. You build that future brick by brick, day by day, through every action, decision, and interaction.

Don't expect things to just fall into place. Relationships don't work that way. The moment you stop nurturing them, they begin to wither. The moment you let your standards slide, you risk losing what you've built. Consistently showing up as the man you aspire to be isn't a one-time effort. It's a continuous process. You can't afford to be passive about it. You need to take ownership of your actions, your role, and your responsibilities.

The journey to becoming a man worthy of respect and admiration isn't easy. If it were, everyone would do it. It requires self-discipline, focus, and a deep sense of integrity. But it's worth it. When you embrace these principles, you're not just bridging the divide between who you are and who you want to become—you're transcending it. You're transforming into a man who doesn't just talk about the life he wants—he builds it, step by step, day by day.

Start today. Don't wait for the perfect moment or for the stars to align. Handle your responsibilities. Take care of yourself. Lead with integrity. Make these principles non-negotiable. The future you deserve isn't something that's just handed to you—it's something you earn. And the work starts now. Every day you show up as the man you aspire to be, you create the life you deserve. Every choice you make shapes your future. So, if you want respect, love, and admiration, start building it today, through the actions you take, the words you speak, and the life you lead.

You don't need to wait for a perfect moment. The moment is now. Begin with these principles, and watch how your world transforms. You're the architect of your future, and it all begins with the man you choose to be today.

Chapter 6:
Unmasking the Illusions:
The Realities of Modern Relationships

I've always been a straight shooter—no fluff, no sugarcoating. And the truth, as uncomfortable as it might be, is that the dynamic between men and women has changed— and not for the better. We've lost something along the way. Something steady. Something sacred.

I look at relationships now and can't help but compare them to what I witnessed growing up. My grandmother was the heartbeat of her family. She worked 12-hour shifts in a factory, came home, cooked, cleaned, and held the household together—all without asking for applause. It wasn't about being praised; it was about doing what needed to be done. My grandfather pulled his weight, too—but in a different way. Their roles weren't about power—they were about purpose.

Today, women want independence, careers, and financial freedom—and I fully support that. Progress is a good thing. But somewhere in the pursuit of that freedom, something essential has been lost. Too often, I've seen relationships where the spirit of the relationship is replaced by a sense of entitlement. Where love is expected, but not given in equal measure. Where effort feels one-sided. And when that happens, resentment creeps in—slowly but surely.

I've watched good men—providers, protectors, emotionally available men—give everything they have, only to be worn down over time. Not by life, but by love that lacked reciprocity. I've seen them shrink into versions of themselves that barely resemble who they once were. And ironically, some of the same women who say they want strength, confidence, and leadership from a man will later resent him for possessing those exact qualities. They try to soften him, reshape him—only to find he's no longer the man they fell for in the first place.

I've seen this pattern unfold time and again—and it's not just a one-off situation. It's a cycle. A quiet erosion of respect for masculine energy. Somewhere along the way, the image of strong, steady, decisive men shifted from being admirable to being something to criticize. More and more, men are being encouraged to step back, to soften themselves, to be less—not because they've failed, but because strength itself is now seen as a threat.

But that kind of dynamic? It doesn't serve anyone. Not the man. Not the woman. Not the relationship.

To be clear, I believe wholeheartedly in strong, capable women. I support women chasing ambition, building careers, and making their mark. But when we come home—when we step into that shared space—it's not about competing goals anymore. It's about collaboration. Companionship. Building something together. That doesn't mean falling into some outdated version of roles. It means understanding each other's value. Pulling weight where it's needed. No scoreboard. No resentment. Just balance.

If she's out there grinding, I'll handle what needs to be handled at home. If I'm the one working late, I hope she's doing the same. Not out of obligation, but because we've got each other's backs. That's the kind of synergy relationships need. And too many couples today are missing it.

What worries me most is how often I see men pulling away from leadership in their own homes—not because they can't lead, but because they've been convinced they shouldn't. That leadership is somehow oppressive. That showing up as the steady hand, the provider—not just financially but emotionally and physically—is outdated. But a relationship without structure drifts. It loses its center. And when men shrink themselves to avoid conflict, everyone loses.

But let's not pretend this is all on men. Respect is a shared responsibility. And here's something many overlook: most men crave respect even more than love. When a man feels disrespected—when his efforts, loyalty, or presence are dismissed—it breaks something inside him. And it's a two-way street. You can't demand respect without giving it. You can't receive it without earning it.

Ladies, if your man shows up—consistently, honestly, and with integrity—and you withhold respect, don't be surprised when he stops offering it in return. We all want to feel seen and valued. And when neither person feels that, you don't just have tension—you have two people slowly pulling away from one another.

This is where the "nice guy" trap comes in. Too many men think that being endlessly agreeable and never speaking up will keep the peace. But peace without honesty is just quiet resentment. And despite what some women say, they don't want a man who disappears into passivity. They want someone who's confident. Who knows who he is. Who can lead with strength and love, not fear and silence.

A man who abandons his identity to make himself more likable doesn't gain admiration—he loses it. And often, he ends up losing the very relationship he was trying so hard to preserve.

That's why I believe so deeply in balance. If you're out in the world chasing goals and building something meaningful—I respect that. Truly. But when you step into a relationship, it's no longer just about personal victories. It's about building something together. It's not about rigid roles—it's about rhythm. About figuring out what works and doing it with intention.

In a healthy relationship, both people contribute. Both are valued for what they bring. And while it doesn't always matter what that contribution is, it does matter that it's understood, appreciated, and aligned with a shared vision. Whether people like to admit it or not, men still have a responsibility to lead that charge—not in dominance, but in direction. Not to control, but to create clarity, structure, and steadiness.

What's missing in so many relationships today isn't necessarily tradition. It's respect. It's understanding. It's a shared commitment to the vision of what a relationship should be—not just what each person wants it to be in the moment.

If I could offer one piece of advice to my own son or daughter, it would be this: strong relationships are not accidents. They are built. Day by day. With intention, with patience, and with effort. Love isn't a shortcut. It's the starting point. What matters more is what you do with that love—how you nurture it, how you show up during the hard seasons, and how you choose each other even when it's not easy or convenient.

That means taking responsibility. On both sides. A lasting relationship is never a one-person job. And yet, I see more and more people waiting for joy to arrive, as if a great life and a loving companionship are things they're owed—

not things they have to work for. That mindset will ruin more relationships than infidelity ever could. Because entitlement slowly rots the foundation from within.

And let's be honest—entitlement shows up on both sides, but I've seen a particular kind growing louder lately. Some women have been fed the belief that they should get everything they want—simply for existing. They see another woman in a thriving relationship and ask, "Why don't I have that?" instead of "What did she do to build that?" But they're missing is the story behind the scenes—the late nights, the disagreements, the compromise, the patience, the forgiveness. The work.

If you're unhappy in your relationship, and your first thought is to look for happiness in someone else's arms, you're already chasing the wrong solution. Sure, it might feel good for a while to be with someone who doesn't get under your skin. But true happiness? That's an inside job. If you're not willing to dig deep and ask why things aren't working—if you're not putting in the effort with your spouse—you'll end up carrying the same wounds into the next relationship, and the one after that.

I get it—leaving seems easier. Especially when social media is telling you that walking away is a form of self-love. You see women online proclaiming, "Leave the good guy," like that's the badge of honor now. But here's the truth most won't admit: behind those curated clips and carefully worded captions, a lot of those people are miserable. Behind the phone, behind the camera—they're carrying regret, loneliness, and disappointment.

Think about the last time you saw someone truly happy posting a video telling the world how fulfilled they were. I'll wait.

You didn't. Because people who are genuinely happy don't need the internet's validation. They're too busy living. Too grounded to chase dopamine from strangers who only know what they choose to show.

Success—whether in a career or a relationship—doesn't just show up. It's earned. It's the quiet result of two people choosing each other, day after day, especially when it's inconvenient. Especially when they don't feel like it.

And one of the most essential parts of that work? Communication. Real, intentional, honest communication—not just unloading emotions and hoping the other person figures it out, but actually listening. Hearing your spouse. Sitting with what they say. Responding with care instead of defensiveness.

Too often, conversations become emotional battlegrounds. And look, your feelings matter. Of course they do. But in a relationship, only focusing on how you feel is a dead end. If both people are too busy trying to be heard, but neither is truly listening, no one gets anywhere. It's not about winning the argument or proving who hurts more. It's about finding a way forward together.

That's what lasting love is built on. Not just chemistry. Not just affection. But the willingness to stay at the table. To talk, to listen, to stretch yourself toward understanding—even when it's uncomfortable. Especially then. That's how you protect something worth keeping.

One of the biggest challenges in relationships today is the idea that personal feelings are the same as facts. They're not. Just because something feels true doesn't mean it is true. That kind of thinking—where emotion replaces reality—can quietly destroy a relationship.

I've seen it happen: people become so locked into how they feel that they lose the ability to see what's real. If they don't like something, they label it wrong. If they're uncomfortable with someone, they assume that person must be toxic. But feelings—while valid—aren't always accurate. They shift. They're shaped by stress, by trauma, by fatigue, by past wounds. Truth doesn't move like that. Truth holds steady.

That ability to step back—to separate emotion from fact—isn't cold or detached. It's maturity. Its strength. And it will serve you not just in love, but in every area of life.

This isn't just about relationships. It's how we navigate the world. Too many people hold on to opinions as if they're gospel, never questioning where they came from or whether they're rooted in anything solid. It happens in politics, in social issues, and in the way we judge each other.

But here's the bottom line: if you can't tell the difference between what you feel and what is real, you're going to have a hard time building anything that lasts— especially love.

Here's something I want you to hold onto: the ability to think clearly—to step outside your emotions and see things as they are—is one of the most powerful skills you'll ever develop. That doesn't mean ignoring how you feel. Emotions matter. But they should inform your thinking, not replace it. When you learn to find that balance, your decisions improve, your relationships grow stronger, and you avoid a whole lot of unnecessary heartache.

So many relationships break down not because of betrayal or abuse—but because people get trapped in their own emotional feedback loop. Every disagreement becomes about who feels what, instead of what's actually happening. But when you learn to pause, breathe, and look at the situation with a bit of distance, something incredible happens: you gain clarity. And with clarity comes growth. You start to see where you've fallen short, where your spouse might be struggling, and what needs to change to move forward.

Without that clarity, you're stuck in a fog—arguing in circles, taking everything personally, and missing the real issues hiding underneath the noise.

And this is the skill so many of us need to strengthen: the ability to cut through emotional static and focus on what truly matters. If you can't separate your feelings from the facts—if every conversation turns into a battlefield because emotions always take the wheel—you won't build something that lasts. You'll build something that spins. And eventually, spins out.

Here's the hard truth: reality doesn't shift just because it's uncomfortable. It doesn't bend to make room for denial. The sooner you face it, the stronger you become—and the stronger your relationship becomes.

Which brings me to a modern threat that's eroding relationships more than most people realize: social media. Specifically? TikTok.

I'm not saying every piece of content is harmful. But after just a few minutes on that app, it's clear how much damage is being done. What's being sold isn't wisdom—it's fantasy. Performances for likes. Soundbites posing as truth. Entire lifestyles curated for clicks. And people—especially younger women—are internalizing this version of reality without asking the most important question: Is any of this real?

I scroll and see it constantly—clip after clip of women declaring they left their husbands, claiming they've "never been happier." And maybe some of them are. But a lot of what you're seeing is projection. A performance. A carefully filtered version of life that skips over the pain, the loneliness, and the regret that often follow. They tell you the grass is greener. What they don't tell you is that it still needs mowing—and sometimes it's just astroturf.

Happiness doesn't come from running. It doesn't come from ghosting responsibility or blaming your spouse every time life gets hard. And it sure doesn't come from taking half of someone's assets and expecting that to fill a void. That's not how fulfillment works. That's how resentment grows.

And yes, I know—this isn't just a one-sided issue. Men walk away from families, too. Some convince themselves they'll be happier alone, free from the pressure of commitment. But let's look at the data: nearly 75% of divorces are initiated by women.

Now, let me be clear—if a relationship is toxic, if there's abuse, neglect, or repeated betrayal, walking away is not only understandable, it's necessary. No one should stay in harm's way. Ever. That's not what this conversation is about.

What I'm talking about are the relationships that aren't broken—just bruised. The ones where effort has gone missing, but love hasn't. The ones where two people have stopped showing up, not because they don't care, but because they've forgotten how. These are the relationships that deserve a second look before the door is closed for good.

And in those cases, my question is simple: have you truly given it your all? Have you had the difficult conversations? Have you looked inward instead of outward? Because if you haven't—if you've skipped the work in search of a feeling—there's a good chance you're chasing something that doesn't exist.

A strong relationship isn't about chasing constant highs. It's about building something steady. Something lasting. Something that still feels worth it, even on the hard days. The moment you start believing that happiness is always somewhere else—in someone else—you set yourself up for a lifetime of running. And the further you run, the further you get from the kind of joy that lasts.

Again, let me be crystal clear: no one should stay in a relationship that's abusive or unsafe. That's not strength— that's survival. You leave. You protect yourself. And you don't look back.

But if you're in a relationship that's simply struggling—if it's strained, but salvageable—I urge you to pause before walking away. Because right now, too many people are being sold this idea that the second something doesn't bring you joy, it's time to walk. And social media only fuels that mindset. You're told, "If it doesn't serve you, leave." Or, "If you're not happy, start over."

But here's what they don't show you—the other side of that decision. The nights that feel longer than you expected. The silence. The loneliness. The weight of doing everything on your own. The realization that a new environment doesn't always bring a new emotional state.

Because here's the truth: happiness doesn't come from changing companions. It comes from changing perspective. It's not something you find—it's something you create. It's something you carry into a relationship, not something you extract from it.

And if we lose sight of that, we'll keep running from the very thing we're trying to build.

I know you're smart. You've got the ability to think clearly, to reflect, to step back and ask the right questions. But too often, that inner wisdom gets drowned out—by emotion, by noise, by outside voices that don't know your heart. And instead of asking, "What can I do to make this better?" the easier answer becomes, "This isn't making me happy—so it must be the problem."

But life doesn't work like that. If you're always chasing happiness outside of yourself, you'll spend your whole life searching and never finding. Because happiness doesn't live "out there." It lives in you.

Marriage—and honestly, any real, lasting relationship—isn't about perfection. It's about commitment. It's about choosing someone—flaws and all—and deciding that this is your person. It's about building something that can weather life's storms, not just enjoy the sunny days. Because the truth is, no matter who you're with, there will be hard seasons. Bad days. Misunderstandings. And still, the strongest relationships are built on this simple decision: I'm not leaving when it gets hard.

And this is what I need you to understand: happiness is your responsibility. It is not your spouse's job to make you happy—just like it's not your job to carry that burden for them. You can share joy with someone, sure. But your sense of fulfillment? That comes from the inside. The moment you stop expecting someone to "complete" you, and start owning your own joy—that's when you become truly ready to love and be loved in a lasting way.

So if you've made a commitment, then honor it. Show up. Be present. Be willing to listen, to grow, to fight for what matters. Love isn't about grand gestures or Instagram-worthy moments—it's about the little things. The daily choices. The effort when no one's watching.

And please—don't fall for the lie that happiness is something someone else hands you. It isn't. It starts and ends with you. When you understand that, not only will your relationships thrive…

You will, too.

Chapter 7:
Modern Dating and Male Standards

The New Dating Landscape

Dating over 40 isn't just a different game—it's a different sport altogether. Swipe culture, unrealistic expectations, and a total disruption of gender roles have turned what used to be a process of connection into a contest of ego and confusion. And dating at any age—as a man—is often either exhausting or straight-up demoralizing. The difficulty? It hinges on what you're seeking and what you're willing to accept. And here's where most men lose the plot.

Let me put this plainly: a good man isn't looking for a "roommate with benefits." He's not looking to be matched tit-for-tat in a scoreboard relationship. He's looking to lead. To protect. To provide. That doesn't mean he's looking to dominate—it means he's looking to fulfill the role wired into his core. Yet, modern feminism has conditioned women to reject the very qualities in men that they naturally desire when life gets real.

They say they want equality, but what they're measuring is surface-level. Equal pay? Done. Opportunities? Open. Yet equality has been misapplied. Women are not the same as men—physically, emotionally, or mentally. That's not offensive. That's biology. That's reality. And frankly, it's the differences that make men and women fit together so powerfully in the first place.

I've seen this again and again: women chasing the illusion of "equality" while measuring themselves against the wrong metrics. Feminism promised them power but delivered burnout and confusion. It told them to become more like men, then turned around and scolded them for being unhappy. The truth? The best thing about a woman is that she's not a man. And vice versa. That's not inequality. That's equilibrium. Each brings strengths to the relationship that the other doesn't.

You can't have two leaders in a home. That's a recipe for chaos. Someone must take the reins. And in a healthy relationship, that leader should be the man. That doesn't mean a woman doesn't lead in areas where her strengths shine—of course she does. A wise man knows when to step back and when to step up. But the overarching direction, the final say, the compass of the household—it belongs to the man who earns it.

The Dating Apps Deception

Let's talk about the elephant in the digital room: dating apps. They're a marketing scam disguised as a solution. The ads show stunning women smiling into sunsets, implying abundance. But when you're actually in the trenches? That's not what you see. Not even close.

Most men are swiping through profile after profile of women who haven't invested in themselves, physically or emotionally. Meanwhile, they demand that the man be fit, stable, adventurous, financially successful, emotionally available—and tall. Always tall. The hypocrisy is staggering.

And then there's the language. Profiles packed with feminist slogans: "I'm independent," "I don't need a man," "I want a man who can handle a strong woman," "fierce," and so on. These buzzwords are red flags, not selling points. They scream, "I'm ready for a fight, not a relationship." It's exhausting, and it's a turn-off.

Here's the truth: men need women, and women need men. Anyone pretending otherwise is living in a fantasy. Yes, I can cook, clean, do my own laundry, fix a leaky faucet, or gut a damn kitchen. Need help moving a couch? I'll call one of my boys. But what I can't get from a buddy is what a woman brings to the relationship that no man ever could—her softness, her emotional depth, her intuition, her care, her touch, her presence.

You can't buy that on TaskRabbit. You can't replicate it with a dog. You can't substitute it with porn or podcasts. You either have it in your life or you don't—and when you do, it changes everything.

Why Standards Matter

So let me ask you: what are your standards? Not your preferences—your standards. Who are you willing to build with? Who are you willing to lead? What kind of woman do you allow into your life and into your space? Because if she doesn't believe in gender roles—traditional ones—you need to move on. Fast.

I'm not saying a woman should be barefoot in the kitchen. I'm saying if she doesn't respect what a man provides—protection, provision, structure, direction—then you're in a no-win situation. You'll be negotiating your masculinity every damn day.

Too many men lower their standards out of scarcity. They stay in the game too long with women who challenge their values instead of complementing them. Why? Because they're afraid of being alone. Let me make this crystal clear: a man with standards might be alone from time to time, but he's never lonely. He's just making room for something real.

Modern dating has created an imbalance between what men offer and what they get in return. You're expected to show up whole, strong, emotionally intelligent, financially capable, sexually dominant, and physically fit. But what are you receiving back? A woman who brings emotional chaos, unresolved trauma, and a demand list that reads like a CEO's job description? That's not equilibrium. That's exploitation.

You are not a utility. You are not an emotional punching bag. You are not an ATM. You are a man, and you need to start acting like one when it comes to your standards. Demand more. Require more. Lead with clarity and strength.

Younger Women and Compatibility

There's a scene in the 2014 film The Little Death that captures something many men have felt but rarely articulate. It's raw, it's unfiltered, and whether it came from truth or a lie, the impact is real. The woman asks about the man's affair partner and says, "She's not younger than me, skinnier than me, or prettier than me. Then why couldn't it just be me?" The man responds, "Because she's softer than you. She's quieter than you. She doesn't yell at me. She doesn't call me an idiot or tell me to shut up all the time. She's nice to me. And she doesn't make me feel like the only thing stopping her from being happy is me."

Let that sink in.

She was focused on physical comparisons. He was focused on emotional reality.

Her looks weren't the issue. Her behavior was. The other woman brought him something that too many men quietly crave—peace. Not performance. Not perfection. Just peace.

Even though, in the context of the film, the man's affair was a fabrication, that doesn't make his words any less honest. It reveals something most men are never given permission to say out loud: what truly draws a man in isn't a flat stomach or a flawless face. It's how he feels in your presence. Is he respected? Is he heard? Is he safe from the constant drip of criticism and emotional volatility?

Now, to be clear, the woman in that scene wasn't even younger. But the traits he described—softness, kindness, respect, emotional calm—are often found more readily in younger women. That's not a rule, but it is a trend. Why? Because younger women haven't always been conditioned by years of resentment, entitlement, or competition with men. They're more willing to bring joy, energy, and cooperation into the dynamic. They still see relationships as an opportunity to build, not a battlefield to win.

Men who date younger women are often accused of wanting control. That narrative is tired—and false. A man who is grounded in his masculine frame isn't looking to control anyone. He's looking to lead a woman who wants to be led. If the dynamic is healthy, there's no power struggle. There's flow. The masculine leads, the feminine responds, and neither feels the need to compete for the steering wheel. That's not hierarchy. That's equilibrium.

I've heard every argument about this. "Older men go for younger women because they're easy to manipulate." No. They go for women who still want to be women— feminine, agreeable, supportive, playful, and kind. When a man finds that, he doesn't have to mold it. He doesn't have to fight for it. It's already present.

This doesn't mean men don't care about looks. Of course, attraction matters. It's the ignition spark, not the engine. What keeps a man there—what makes him choose you again and again—is how you show up emotionally. A woman's beauty might turn heads. Her presence either builds a man—or slowly breaks him down.

A man doesn't want to come home from the stress of the world only to walk into a house full of masculine energy. He doesn't want a verbal sparring companion. He doesn't want to defend his decisions, justify his preferences, or constantly answer to someone who treats him like a subordinate. He wants softness. He wants quiet respect. He wants warmth.

This isn't about oppression—it's about peace.

When a woman stays in her feminine frame—especially at home—it restores something inside the man. It anchors him. It reminds him why he works hard, why he fights, and why he leads. She becomes his equilibrium. And he, in turn, steps fully into the role of protector, provider, and decision-maker—not out of duty, but out of desire.

So let's kill the lie that men are shallow fools chasing youth and tight skin. Yes, youth brings certain things naturally—energy, vitality, enthusiasm—but it's not the whole story. Men are not just visual creatures. We're visceral creatures. We respond to tone, to softness, to support. If younger women often embody these traits more consistently, then that's not a man's fault—it's simply what he values showing up in a form that hasn't been hardened by the world.

And if you're wondering why a younger woman would want an older man in the first place—consider this: maybe she wants leadership. Maybe she's tired of boys who look good on paper but can't hold the frame. Maybe she wants security. Maybe she wants masculine direction. And maybe, just maybe, she respects a man who knows exactly who he is.

The Double Standard of "Man shaming"

Scroll through social media long enough and you'll hear it: the woman's checklist for a man—six feet tall, six-inch penis, six-figure income. That's the "standard." Sounds catchy. Until you realize it's a statistical joke.

Let's break it down.

Only about 14.5% of men in the U.S. are over six feet tall. Roughly 16% make over $100K annually, and the median income for male workers in this country is nearly $68,000.00. And as for that six-inch benchmark? The average penis size is 5.17 inches. Fewer than 8% of men cross that line. So the likelihood of a woman meeting a man who checks all three boxes? About 0.16%. That's less than one percent. You'd have better odds of hitting a small jackpot in Vegas.

This isn't just about numbers—it's about the absurdity of expectations. Because while women are allowed to say things like "I won't date a man under six feet" or mock a guy with "small dick energy," men are expected to just take it. But the moment a man says, "I don't date overweight women" or "I prefer a feminine woman who doesn't yell," all hell breaks loose.

The hypocrisy is loud—and it's exhausting.

You've seen the clips. A man gets mocked on TikTok for not ordering cheese on a burger to save money. Another gets called "the ick" for trying to protect a woman from oncoming traffic. These aren't red flags. These are desperate attempts to shame men for being men. And men are checking out because of it.

Let me be clear: most women aren't like this. But the ones who are? They're damaging themselves more than anyone else. They're chasing a fantasy—one built on filters, entitlement, and the delusion that a man's worth comes down to height, bank account, and what's in his pants. That's not a standard. That's a cartoon.

A man's value isn't found in inches or income alone. It's found in character, commitment, and how he shows up every day. You think a "short king" can't provide, protect, or lead a household? Think again. But the shallow ones will walk right past him—because their fantasy didn't come gift-wrapped in six feet of height.

Let's address the elephant in the room. Height and penis size are not things a man can change. If you reject a man over that, fine—it's your right. But don't cry foul when a man doesn't want to date you because of your weight. That's not hate. That's reciprocity. And guess what? You can change your weight. He can't stretch himself taller or rewrite his genetics.

So let's stop pretending this is about fairness. This is about a double standard that gives women the freedom to insult, shame, and reject men based on things they cannot control, while demanding unconditional acceptance in return.

Men are allowed to have standards. Period.

If a man doesn't want to date someone with kids, that's his right. If he doesn't want to marry a career-focused woman who won't cook or clean, that's his choice. If he's not attracted to a woman who doesn't match his ideal body type or combative, that's personal preference, not misogyny.

Yet every time a man articulates those preferences, women lose their minds. It's as if men aren't supposed to be selective, like their standards are offensive simply because they exist. That's not equality. That's narcissism.

Let me say this clearly: you don't have to like a man's standards—but you damn sure have to respect his right to have them. The same way you expect him to respect yours.

This double standard has been a quiet undercurrent for years, but now it's right in our faces. The dating market is broken because women are told they should aim for the top 1% while simultaneously being offended if they're not chosen themselves. That's not a recipe for love. That's a recipe for bitterness.

Here's the reality—men and women are different. We always have been. And that's a good thing. But if we want meaningful connections, we have to stop pretending that one side's preferences are valid while the other side's are "shallow." Standards apply both ways, and if we want equilibrium, we need to stop the man-shaming and start owning our choices.

You want a six-foot man with six figures and six inches? Cool. Just don't act surprised when he wants a woman who's fit, feminine, kind, and low drama. You don't get to play the game without being in it.

Just food for thought.

The Opt-Out Movement

Some men have stopped playing the game altogether. Not because they hate women, not because they're broken—but because they're tired. Tired of the double standards. Tired of the unrealistic expectations. Tired of feeling like showing up as a man isn't enough unless he checks every box on a fantasy list created by people who have no intention of meeting him halfway.

Dating today, especially through apps, can feel like a full-time job with no pay and no respect. What used to be a path to connection has become a maze of entitlement, superficial checklists, and landmines called "icks." One day it's your iced latte, the next it's your political views. Maybe she doesn't like that you're bald. Maybe it's your white sneakers. Or maybe—God forbid—you tried to protect her from oncoming traffic and that made you look "weak."

This is the madness men are walking away from.

And I don't blame them.

Ask yourself this: Why should a man subject himself to constant judgment, performative femininity, and emotional whiplash just for the chance to maybe be tolerated? Why jump through hoops for someone who sees him as an accessory, not an anchor?

More men are asking that question—and more men are walking away.

The message has been loud and clear for years: "Don't approach women." So men stopped. You may argue you never said that, but silence isn't exactly helping your case. If you want men to approach, speak louder than the women who treat every advance like harassment. Because right now, those voices are dominating the narrative—and men are listening.

Approaching a woman today is like walking into a minefield. The risk of rejection is expected—that's life. But the brutality? That's something else. Some women don't just say "no"—they say it with venom, with mockery, with public humiliation. That's not strength. That's cruelty dressed in insecurity. If the roles were reversed, you'd want dignity and kindness. So why not extend the same?

Women speak about empathy often, but where is it when a man puts himself out there? Where is it when he opens his mouth and gets laughed at before he finishes a sentence? You can't demand grace and then serve none in return.

Men have learned. Not just to stop approaching, but to stop engaging. Not out of weakness, but self-respect.

They've turned their focus inward. Toward purpose. Toward discipline. Toward building something meaningful in their lives that doesn't require approval, acceptance, or validation from someone who sees dating as an opportunity to audition suitors like reality TV contestants.

And here's the part that needs to be said, whether it stings or not:

You're not inviting a man into your life. He's inviting you into his.

He's the builder. He's the protector. He's the leader. That role isn't a threat. It's a structure. It's stability. It's what makes a woman feel secure, provided she actually wants to feel that way.

Masculine men are not drawn to competition. Especially not with the woman they're dating. He's not interested in fighting for the steering wheel in his own house. That's not equality. That's friction. And friction burns a relationship down from the inside out.

When a woman insists on leading, challenges every decision, and resists direction just for the sake of it, it doesn't make her strong—it makes her incompatible. There's nothing attractive about a constant power struggle in the home. And no, I'm not saying a woman shouldn't speak her mind. I'm saying if you have to dominate the relationship to feel secure, you're not ready for a masculine man.

Now, I get it. Some women feel like they had to lead because the man in their life wasn't stepping up. That's a valid frustration. But let me be clear—when a woman is forced to carry the masculine because the man has abdicated it, no one is happy. She resents it. He resents himself. And the entire dynamic collapses.

Equilibrium comes when each person brings their natural strengths to the relationship—not when both are wrestling for control.

Men are tired of that wrestle. So they're opting out. Not because they can't win. But because the prize no longer seems worth it. And unless something shifts—unless more women start honoring the masculine instead of competing with it—the exodus will continue.

You can call them cowards. You can label them bitter. But you'd be wrong. These men aren't running away. They're choosing peace.

And peace, in this world, is priceless.

Later-Life Male Value

Let's kill the myth right now—men do not lose value with age. In fact, if a man plays it right, he gains it. Purpose sharpens. Confidence deepens. Finances stabilize. Looks? They evolve. Not everyone can be a cover model, but presence and composure go a long way. A man who takes care of himself—physically, emotionally, and financially— doesn't age out. He ages up.

There's a reason you see men in their 40s and 50s with women a decade or more younger. No, it's not just about money. It's about confidence—the kind that can't be faked. You've seen it before: a shorter, average-looking guy walking into a room with a stunning woman. You wonder how he pulled that off. The answer's simple—he believed he could.

Confidence is magnetic. A man who walks with purpose and speaks with certainty doesn't chase—he attracts. Women respond to that. And while society keeps telling men to "settle down" before they hit their prime, what they're really saying is "don't realize how powerful you're becoming."

Don't listen to that noise.

If you've built yourself—if you've stayed focused, kept your values tight, stayed in shape, built your income, and sharpened your mindset—you have options. You are not obligated to settle just because the calendar says you're supposed to. You set your own timeline. You choose what you accept. And you determine what's worthy of your time, your leadership, and your love.

Reclaiming Dating with Clarity

Dating isn't broken. But your standards might be.

Men need to stop apologizing for wanting more—and better. That's not arrogance. That's called discernment. But let's be clear: you don't get to demand respect until you've earned it. Respect is the price of admission in any meaningful connection. Friendship. Marriage. Flirtation. Family. It doesn't matter what the title is—if respect's not present, the relationship has no foundation.

You respect the people you value. If you don't, then why are they still in your life?

Too many men tolerate behavior they hate just because the woman is attractive. You meet someone, you're drawn in, and suddenly you're ignoring every red flag waving in your face. You convince yourself it's not a big deal. But deep down, you know better. That's not strength. That's settling.

At some point, you have to be honest with yourself: What are your non-negotiables? What kind of behavior are you never willing to tolerate? And are you brave enough to walk away when it shows up?

For me, it's simple. Rudeness to wait staff? I don't care how pretty you are—you're done. That behavior doesn't belong to masculinity or femininity. It belongs to people who lack empathy. The restaurant could be on fire and backed up to the walls, and I still expect you to treat those workers with respect. They're hustling. They're human. And if you can't grasp that, I'm out. No second chance. No compromise.

That's what standards look like.

Now, let's talk about masculine behavior—chivalry. If you've found a man who still opens your door, walks you to your car, pulls your chair out, and places himself between you and oncoming traffic, pay attention. That's not a gimmick. That's masculinity in motion. That's a man raised with a code.

And yet, today, men are told to hide that part of themselves. Feminism took chivalry out back and shot it— then cried foul when men stopped showing up like gentlemen. That's not progress. That's confusion.

I open the door for women. Always will. Not for applause. Not for gratitude. It's just who I am. It's how I was raised. I don't care if you're a stranger, my wife, or someone I'll never see again—I'm holding that damn door. Because respect isn't conditional. It's a habit.

Men, reclaim your standards. Women, respect the men who hold them. Stop demanding perfection while rejecting the qualities that define masculinity.

Dating doesn't have to be chaotic.

But it does have to be intentional.

Stop chasing chemistry and start evaluating character. Stop pretending men and women are the same. We're not. We never will be. And that's the entire point.

When a man steps into his full value—when he leads, protects, provides, and lives by his own code—he doesn't need to chase anyone. He simply chooses who gets to come along for the ride.

And that, gentlemen, is what modern dating should look like.

Chapter 8:
The Lies We're Sold and the Truth We Keep Ignoring

I've spent a great deal of time in this book laying out what I believe are the key factors driving a wedge between men and women. One point remains at the top of my list: modern feminism. Not the original wave that pushed for voting rights and equal opportunity. I'm talking about the current iteration—the one that distorts communication, demonizes masculinity, and reframes every interaction through a lens of hostility and suspicion.

One of the most misrepresented concepts in today's gender discourse is submission. Say the word, and it is as if someone just demanded a woman grovel at a man's feet. The emotional backlash is immediate. Women bristle, men retreat, and no one takes the time to unpack what the word actually means. It's not about obedience. It's not about control. And it damn sure isn't about treating anyone like a pet.

Let me be absolutely clear: submission, in a healthy relationship dynamic, is about mutual respect, not domination. But I don't blame women for reacting the way they do. I blame the cultural narratives that have equated traditional gender roles with oppression. I blame the talking heads who feed the lie that every man with standards is a tyrant in disguise. And yes, I understand the frustration behind movements like MGTOW. When men feel like the rules are rigged against them, when respect and reciprocity are off the table, walking away becomes a logical—if unfortunate—response.

This issue doesn't exist in a vacuum. It's reinforced, amplified, and poisoned by online platforms that masquerade as "communities" but function more like digital echo chambers. I've come to the conclusion that most of us would be better off stepping away from these digital traps altogether—TikTok, Instagram, Facebook, Reddit—you name it. These platforms are not tools for connection; they're feeding tubes for discontent.

The content pushed through these channels isn't neutral. It's designed to provoke, radicalize, and pull people into ideological corners. I scroll through these apps and see the same toxic narratives over and over again. "Leave the good guy and chase your own happiness." "You deserve more." "If he's not giving you butterflies every second, he's the wrong one."

Let me make this crystal clear: you will not find fulfillment outside yourself. That emptiness you feel? It doesn't get solved by switching relationships. It doesn't go away because you left someone who was decent, loyal, and committed. If your own identity is fractured, the best person in the world will still disappoint you. I've said it before, and I'll say it again—your happiness comes from within, and the minute you outsource it, you lose control over your own life.

Online spaces love to celebrate destructive choices under the guise of enablement. But here's what happens when you push back: you're labeled judgmental, toxic, or out of touch. Say something like "you left a good man because you were bored," and prepare to be attacked. You'll hear things like "you don't know the full story" or "you're not in her shoes." That's true. But when someone posts their life on the internet, they're inviting public feedback. If you only tell one side, and then expect people to read between the lines in your favor, you're not being honest—you're being manipulative.

These forums are not places for open dialogue. They are spaces where only the "approved" narratives are allowed to live. Anything that contradicts the echo gets shouted down. That's not growth—that's groupthink. And if you're chasing validation instead of truth, you're never going to evolve.

Let me offer you a radical solution: keep your private life private. Not everything needs to be broadcasted. Not every thought deserves a platform. I know that concept feels foreign in a world obsessed with sharing, but ask yourself—what's the return on constantly putting your life out there for public consumption? I run a podcast. I have a YouTube channel. I talk about masculinity, leadership, responsibility—because that's what I know. But I do not talk about my family. I do not post about my personal relationships. That's sacred ground. Not everything is content. Some things are meant to be lived, not posted.

In my coaching practice, I've seen this over and over: people come in looking for answers outside themselves. But here's the truth—they already know the answer. You just have to let them speak long enough, and it eventually comes out. Last night, I spoke with a man who was tangled up in his own thoughts. Fifteen minutes in, he solved his own dilemma. That's the beauty of clarity—it doesn't come from social media. It comes from honest self-reflection.

The internet thrives on chaos and controversy, but real growth doesn't. Real growth happens in quiet moments, in hard conversations, in the mirror. You don't need a trending hashtag to get better. You need discipline, self-awareness, and the willingness to face the truth—even when it's uncomfortable.

So let's stop pretending that your next dopamine hit on TikTok is going to fix your marriage. Let's stop blaming algorithms for choices we made ourselves. And let's start asking harder questions: What am I running from? What truth have I refused to face? Because until you answer those, no amount of likes or shares will give you what you're looking for.

Online platforms have made some progress. Reddit, for example, has taken real steps to shut down spaces that promote open misogyny or misandry. Yet let's not kid ourselves—those mindsets haven't disappeared. They've just shifted into new corners of the internet, hiding behind usernames and encrypted group chats. Same poison, different bottle.

Let me explain the modern incel phenomenon. Incel stands for involuntary celibate, but that definition barely scratches the surface. The incel community, as it exists today, is a twisted, angry corner of the digital world—primarily made up of men who've been rejected, ignored, or humiliated in the dating arena. Many of them are socially withdrawn, lack confidence, and have no meaningful relationships with women. Rather than looking inward, they externalize their failures and pin the blame on women. And that is where the line is crossed—from disappointment to delusion.

Ironically, this movement wasn't even founded by a man. The term *incel* was coined in the 1990s by a Canadian woman who originally created the community as a support space for men and women who were struggling to find romantic connections. It was meant to be a place of encouragement and shared vulnerability—a digital shelter for people trying to make sense of their loneliness. The original founder eventually found love and moved on, but the space she created did not. Over time, it morphed into a toxic enclave where self-pity evolved into hatred.

Today's incel forums are nothing like what they were meant to be. These spaces are now filled with bitterness, entitlement, and outright hostility toward women. They don't just vent—they weaponize their disappointment. They trade in contempt. And worst of all, some of them have crossed the line into real-world violence. There have been mass shootings carried out by self-identified incels who blamed their failures on "Chads" and "Stacies"—slang terms used to describe attractive, socially successful men and women. In their warped reality, these individuals are responsible for their pain. So instead of fixing their own mindset, they lash out.

Let me be direct: these men are not men. They are broken, angry boys playing victims in a world they don't know how to navigate. Real manhood isn't built on resentment. It's built on self-awareness, responsibility, and discipline. And make no mistake—the incel narrative stains the rest of us. Good men who are doing the work, building themselves up, and treating women with respect often get lumped into the same category simply because they share the same biology. Guilt by association. It's unfair—but it's also reality.

The same thing happens in reverse. Many men, fed up with modern dating dynamics, start to categorize all women based on the worst examples they've encountered. If she ghosted him, used him, lied to him, or manipulated him, suddenly all women are "like that." And just like that, both sides become guilty of the same generalization. One bad experience, one emotional wound, and we paint an entire gender with the same brush.

This is how division becomes the norm. This is how men and women stop seeing each other as human beings and start viewing each other as enemies. The echo chambers of the internet are largely to blame. These platforms encourage us to sit in our pain instead of doing the hard work of growth. They provide sympathy when what we need is truth. They hand out excuses when what we need is responsibility.

I'm not here to dismiss real pain. Rejection hurts. Loneliness can crush a person. But pain does not give anyone the right to turn hateful or destructive. You do not get to give up on personal growth and start blaming the world. Life doesn't reward that mindset. Society certainly won't. And as a coach, I refuse to validate it.

Here is the hard truth: If you're not getting what you want in life—whether it's a relationship, respect, or success—it's on you to fix that. No one owes you a date. No one owes you their affection. The moment you start blaming women, society, or biology for your shortcomings, you've already lost. Because you've given up the one thing that separates men from boys—ownership.

And to the men who think it's unfair that we are all judged by the worst of us—welcome to what women have been dealing with for decades. Both men and women have suffered from stereotypes and assumptions. But doubling down on bitterness only proves the stereotype right. What changes that? Accountability. Growth. Grit. That's the path forward—not message boards full of self-pity and rage.

So, if you are feeling overlooked, rejected, or misunderstood—good. That pain is your wake-up call. Use it. Build something out of it. Transform it into strength instead of resentment. That is what real men do.

Let's call it what it is—we are addicted to social media. Not in a light, casual way either. I mean hardwired, thumb-scrolling, dopamine-chasing, echo-chamber addiction. And it is costing us something we cannot afford to lose: independent thought.

I see it constantly. People parroting soundbites, regurgitating headlines, or blindly reposting some influencer's latest "truth" without once asking themselves if it even makes sense. What blows my mind is how many people lack a personal opinion about the opposite sex, politics, relationships, or the world around them. They don't form beliefs—they absorb them. No filter. No friction. Just blind consumption.

We've traded logic for likes.

We've raised a generation so flooded by curated media and 24-hour outrage cycles that many cannot step back long enough to ask a basic question: Is this right? And if not, why do I believe it's wrong? Instead of wrestling with truth, they fall in line. They conform. And they call it awareness. What they're really doing is outsourcing their thinking to the loudest voice in the room.

The fear of challenging anything—even within themselves—is so great that they'll align with whatever ideology sounds most comforting or most "accepted." Challenge feminism? Impossible. Question what you've been taught since childhood? Unthinkable. Reconsider a belief that's shaped your identity? Too uncomfortable. If you cannot question who you are or why you believe what you do, how can anyone expect you to challenge anything outside of yourself?

Let me be real with you: beliefs do not equal truth. Beliefs are formed—often by repetition, emotion, environment, and habit. And if you never interrogate your beliefs, you're not living. You're just programmed. The number of adults who have never questioned the ideologies spoon-fed to them by parents, peers, schools, or media is staggering. You ask them why they believe something, and all they can offer is a shrug or a recycled slogan.

Let me give you a personal example.

I spent 20 years in the military. For two decades, punctuality wasn't just expected—it was drilled into me. Being early was the rule. Not five minutes early. Fifteen. Showing up "on time" was considered late. That mindset became part of who I was. Even after retirement, I carried that urgency into civilian life. I hated lateness. I saw it as disrespectful, undisciplined, and frankly, rude.

But here's where the shift happened—I started to ask myself why I felt that way.

Was being five minutes late to a casual dinner truly disrespectful? Was someone a lesser human because they hit traffic or misjudged the time? No. But that's what I believed—not because it was true, but because I was trained to believe it.

That belief served me in the military, where timeliness meant operational success. But in everyday life? It started to create unnecessary stress. I'd get irritated waiting for someone. I'd judge people for running behind. Eventually, I had to confront the belief head-on: Was this a personal standard rooted in character, or was it an overgrown military reflex I hadn't unlearned yet?

Turns out, it was the latter.

Now, I still respect people's time. I still believe in showing up prepared. But I also recognize that life happens. Being five minutes late to a barbecue doesn't make someone undisciplined. It makes them human. That realization didn't come from a book or a podcast—it came from questioning something I had accepted for years without challenge. It came from being honest enough to admit: I don't need this belief anymore.

And that's the point. Most people never do that.

They never stop to evaluate the origin of their beliefs—where they picked them up, why they hold onto them, and whether those beliefs are still serving them. Some beliefs need to be reinforced. Others need to be burned to the ground.

You cannot grow until you learn to challenge your programming.

So ask yourself: Why do I believe what I believe? Who gave me this lens? Who taught me to view men or women a certain way? Who told me success looks like this? Who told me I had to be this kind of person to be respected?

These are the hard questions. But asking them is where transformation begins. Until then, you're not thinking—you're recycling. And no one ever built a meaningful life on borrowed beliefs.

Media, in all its forms, is unreliable at best and manipulative at worst. And no, I'm not only referring to cable news or political commentary. I'm talking about the entire spectrum—social media platforms, legacy networks, digital blogs, and yes, even the "lifestyle" outlets that disguise opinion as truth.

As an entrepreneur, I understand the need to use media. If you want to promote your business or expand your brand, the reach it provides is essential. You play the game because visibility is the price of growth. Even this book has a website, and maybe that's where you bought it from. That's reality. I get that. But acknowledging the necessity of media doesn't mean we should ignore how dangerous it can be when misused.

What I do not understand—what I cannot excuse— is how outright lies make their way into the public narrative and are consumed as if they're gospel truth. Where is the line between opinion and misinformation? And who exactly is holding the fact-checkers accountable? Let's be honest— much of what gets passed around as truth these days is nothing more than manipulated opinion dressed up as moral authority.

I am not even talking strictly about politics—though you could write a library on how distorted that coverage is, no matter where you stand on the aisle. I am talking about the garbage that passes for journalism, the headlines built to divide, and the content designed to spark outrage and clicks, not understanding or truth.

Still, I will always stand behind your right to say it.

The First Amendment is a powerful thing. It gives me the freedom to say what I believe in this book, whether it's popular or not. You're free to agree or disagree. It does not offend me either way. What matters is that I remain consistent, honest, and fair to both men and women, even when I hit nerves.

Both genders have flaws. We are not mirror images—we are polar opposites by design. That difference is not a flaw—it's the foundation of attraction. There's nothing inherently toxic about masculinity, and there's nothing threatening about a woman embracing her feminine nature. What's toxic is pretending otherwise.

Let me break this down clearly: masculinity is not a problem. Femininity is not a weakness. What's problematic is the growing trend of labeling entire genders as dangerous based on the behavior of a few bad actors. Some men are selfish. Some women are manipulative. That does not mean manhood is broken or that womanhood is flawed. It just means some people suck.

But culture has a habit of going too far. One writer, who calls herself "Katie," wrote that working out six days a week is a sign of toxic masculinity. Let that sink in. Apparently, being in shape, staying disciplined, and building physical strength is now something to be ashamed of. According to her, fitness creates a cycle of male dominance that must be eradicated.

That's not just absurd. That's delusional.

I see women in the gym every day grinding just as hard. Is their strength toxic, too? Or is it only toxic when a man does it? This is what happens when we replace truth with ideology. It becomes okay to insult men for doing the very things that have, historically, saved lives, protected families, and built society from the ground up.

Now, I wouldn't even bring up a fringe article like that if it weren't for the fact that it reflects a much larger pattern. You've got mainstream brands like Gillette running entire campaigns on how masculinity is toxic, while selling razors to the very men they're busy insulting. Make it make sense. Alienating your customer base to appear "woke" might score some social points, but it sends a reckless message to the public.

Here's what I want you to consider: when something heavy needs lifting, when someone's life is on the line, when you're facing danger head-on, you're going to want a man who embraces his masculine edge. That instinct to protect, to act decisively, to lead under pressure—that is not toxic. That is essential. Denying that truth is not just foolish—it's dangerous.

This lie has been fed to us for years, starting at a young age. One of the biggest culprits? Disney.

Disney has been shaping perceptions of men and women for generations. Fairy tales sell us a fantasy where the woman is rescued, the man wins her love by groveling, simping, or saving the day, and everyone lives happily ever after. No struggle. No disagreements. No work. Just a perfect ending with fireworks.

It's a beautiful illusion—and a terrible blueprint for reality.

Real relationships don't work that way. Love isn't handed to you in a musical number. It's built. It's challenged. It gets tested over time. But when your model of relationships is based on a cartoon romance where every woman is flawless and every man must earn her approval through self-sacrifice, you're being programmed to fail.

Men start believing they must "prove" their worth to women. Women start believing that a man's job is to endlessly chase and cater to them. Neither role leads to equilibrium. Neither creates strength, respect, or love.

Here is the truth: relationships take work. Not pixie dust. Not a rescue mission. Not blind devotion. Two people must show up as their full selves—committed to honesty, growth, and shared direction. That kind of relationship doesn't make headlines or movies, but it makes families. It builds legacies.

We've been sold a lie. Now it is time to start living the truth.

Let's cut to the chase—addiction to social media is real, and it's not just wasting time; it's shaping belief systems. Worse than that, it's warping how men and women see each other. Every day, we're hit with half-truths, biased rants, and clickbait content about relationships, gender roles, and human nature—and people swallow it whole, no questions asked. If it shows up online, it must be true, right?

That mindset is dangerous. It creates a culture where the loudest story wins, not the most truthful one. You scroll through TikTok or Instagram, and you'll find someone ranting about how all men are trash or that women are just users who manipulate for attention. No nuance. No context. Just blanket blame.

The disturbing part? Most people don't even ask questions.

They see a post—often from someone they've never met—and instantly adopt the opinion as their own. Especially when the speaker fits the narrative they already want to believe. Say it with conviction, add a trending hashtag, and suddenly, you're an expert.

What shocks me is how many grown adults—men and women alike—fall for this. They reach conclusions without hearing both sides, without checking facts, and without any real understanding of the situation. It's the same mentality you see in mob culture: someone gets accused of something, and before the facts are even laid out, the verdict is already in. Guilty until proven innocent. Or worse—guilty even after being proven innocent.

But here's the bigger issue—it's not just adults being misled. It's our kids.

This is where the indoctrination really begins. When I said earlier that people no longer know where their beliefs came from, this is the root. For my generation, the influence started with Disney. We were fed perfect fairytales, unrealistic expectations, and polished ideals of what men and women should be. But for today's kids? It's TikTok, Instagram, YouTube shorts, influencers, pseudo-therapists, and algorithm-driven chaos.

It's not just misinformation—it's identity programming. They're not just learning opinions. They're absorbing ideologies before they're old enough to question them.

I saw this firsthand as a father. When my daughter was in high school, I walked into her school and noticed CNN was being piped in through the TVs. That's not education—that's a broadcast. And it wasn't just the news—social media picked up where the classroom left off. Suddenly, I was competing with the narratives she was seeing and hearing every day. Not because I wanted her to think like me—but because I wanted her to think for herself.

That's the point.

I wasn't trying to indoctrinate her with my views. I was trying to teach her how to develop her own beliefs—based on evidence, logic, and personal conviction, not memes and mob mentality. It's a fight every parent has to face now. And if you don't plant the seed of independent thought early, the world will gladly do it for you.

And what's the result of all this noise?

We've now got young people forming opinions about themselves and the world around them based on repetition, not reflection. If they're not hearing it from schools, they're hearing it from social media. If not from social media, then from their friends—who are just as misinformed. That's a lot of influence to combat if you're not being intentional as a parent, teacher, or mentor.

This constant loop of programming also drives the gender divide deeper. We've all heard the messaging: "Men are the problem," "Masculinity is toxic," "Women don't need men," and "Boss babe or bust." These phrases get recycled until they start sounding like truth, but no one stops to ask: Is this what I actually believe? Or did I just hear it enough times to assume it's valid?

Some people take the bait and run with it, never once asking what they truly want in life or in a relationship. For example, a woman might embrace the "boss babe" lifestyle—and that's her choice. But let's be honest: that lifestyle is not going to align with a man who wants a traditional home life, where he works, and his significant other nurtures the household.

That's not judgment. That's reality.

It's like trying to fit a square peg into a round hole. A man who values tradition will not thrive with a woman who proudly says, "I don't need a man." And a woman who's focused solely on independence and ambition is not going to find contentment with a man who wants a quiet, family-centered life.

Those are fundamental mismatches, and no amount of compromise will erase them.

Yet, instead of recognizing these realities, society pushes the idea that "love conquers all" or that "opposites attract." That's fantasy. Real relationships don't succeed on clichés. They succeed on compatibility, shared values, and clarity about what each person brings to the relationship and expects in return.

Now, I'll explain how to avoid these mismatches— and how to identify what you really want—in a later chapter. But here's your takeaway for now:

Stop letting strangers on the internet tell you what to think about the opposite sex.

Stop repeating things just because you heard them on a screen.

And start asking questions that matter: What do I actually believe? Why do I believe it? And is it still true for me today?

So, how do we fight back?

How do we separate truth from noise, especially in a world where everyone with a smartphone thinks they are an authority on life, love, and relationships?

We start by challenging the beliefs we carry. Every single one of them.

This is not an easy exercise. It takes humility. It takes courage. And frankly, you may need a coach or mentor to help you sift through the beliefs you've absorbed versus the truths you've actually chosen.

Ask yourself this: Why do I believe what I believe about myself? Are you "confident," or have you simply learned to perform confidence for approval? Do you believe you are difficult? Or did someone else label you that, and now you wear it like a badge? Are you convinced you're unworthy—or have you never been shown how to see your worth in the first place?

Most people never pause to ask the hard questions. Instead, they let childhood messages, broken relationships, or social media slogans define their identity.

For example—if you believe you are a "princess," why?

Is that a title your parents used to affirm you? Is it something you were told your whole life until you began expecting others to treat you like royalty, too? And if so—is that belief serving you in adult relationships?

Let me be clear: If a grown woman introduces herself to me as a "princess," I am running the other way. That is not a compliment—it is a red flag. Because it tells me she is holding onto an illusion that likely has no roots in reality. Unless she's got a royal bloodline and a crown to match, I know that belief has been fed to her, not earned.

And here's the kicker: none of us are royalty. Not unless you have an official title—and if you are American, that is off the table. We are people—flawed, evolving, human. And that is more powerful than any fantasy.

What needs to happen is a deep audit of your beliefs—not just about yourself, but about your relationships and the world around you.

Ask: Where did these beliefs come from? Who gave them to me? Are they based in truth or convenience? Are they helping me or holding me back?

This is not about changing everything you believe. It is about making sure the beliefs you hold are actually yours. When you've tested them, examined them, and consciously chosen to keep them—then they belong to you. Otherwise, they belong to someone else.

That includes the content you consume.

Social media has already earned its place on the list of what's eroding society's mental strength—and if you've been paying attention to this chapter, you know I believe it's doing more damage than most people are willing to admit. It's making people lazy thinkers. And if you are not challenging what you see, you are not thinking at all.

Ask yourself: Why am I blindly believing this guy who says all women are toxic? Or this woman who claims every ex she left was a narcissist? Are you really hearing the whole story—or just the part that fits their narrative?

It gets worse when we start comparing ourselves to social media highlights.

You see a woman posing in a bikini on a boat with a fake smile, and you assume she's living the dream. You see a couple on vacation posting their romantic dinner and believe they've got the perfect relationship. What you do not see is the argument they had after the camera shut off, the late nights that led to burnout, or the fact that their relationship is hanging by a thread.

Most of what people show is a manufactured moment—not the full picture. It is a filtered performance for public approval, not a snapshot of truth.

Nobody's showing you the sleepless nights, the rejections, the insecurities, or the mental breakdowns. They're not showing the work. They're not showing the sacrifice. And they sure as hell are not showing the parts that would make them look weak or average.

And yet, you scroll, and you assume they've got it better than you. Stop doing that.

Here is the truth: if someone's life is perfect on social media, they are either lying or they are marketing. Probably both. I can count on one hand—with no fingers—the number of people who post their life authentically, the good and the bad, day in and day out.

Also, remember this: everything you hear online about someone's relationship is one side of the story. There's always another perspective, but you rarely hear it. Every once in a while, you'll see the other person in the relationship respond with a video, trying to correct the record. But those are rare. Most stay silent while strangers attack them in the comments, based on a single-sided post designed to trigger sympathy and outrage.

That goes for men, too. I am seeing an increasing number of men crying on camera about how unfairly they were treated. And sure, some may have a valid reason to share. But ask yourself: Is this the full story? What behavior are we not seeing? You cannot form a sound judgment off one side of the narrative.

So here is my challenge to you: be discerning.

Be skeptical about what you consume online.

Do not be the person who believes life is greener on the digital side of the fence. Life is hard. Relationships are messy. Identity is complicated. And all of that is perfectly normal.

But if you want to rise above the noise, if you want to build a relationship worth having and a life worth living— you must start looking inward.

What do you believe about yourself?

What do you believe about others?

What do you believe about the world?

The answers to those questions will shape every decision you make from this point forward.

Choose wisely.

Chapter 9:
The Line in the Sand Is Yours to Draw

Let's get one thing straight—building a strong, lasting relationship doesn't happen by accident. It takes time. It takes intention. And it takes the emotional maturity to navigate the inevitable rough waters life will send your way.

Those storms will come. Count on it.

You don't get a pass just because you love each other. You don't get immunity because you had a great first year. Love doesn't insulate you from adversity. And if your blueprint for love is based on fairytales or Instagram highlights, let me tell you right now—reality will break you.

Forget what Disney taught you. Life is not a smooth ride. It's unpredictable. It's hard. It will test your patience, your emotional stamina, and your sense of self. And when that happens, especially in a relationship, the temptation to throw in the towel will be real.

Sometimes, that's exactly what needs to happen.

Sometimes, the damage is too deep. The betrayal too severe. The emotional toll too high. In those cases, walking away is not a failure—it's survival. There are situations where one or both individuals reach a point of no return. And even if forgiveness is possible, the dynamic is permanently altered. Trust doesn't always rebuild. Connection doesn't always come back.

That is life. It's messy. It's painful. But it's also yours to manage.

No one else can draw that line for you. Only you can determine when you've had enough—when preserving your peace and protecting your mental health requires stepping away.

However, the goal is not to prepare for failure—it's to build something strong enough that failure becomes unlikely.

And here's how you do that: you build your relationship on truth. You build it on respect, consistent honesty, effective communication, boundaries that are honored—not crossed—and the kind of kindness that doesn't disappear when things get difficult.

Those are not romantic ideals. They are practical requirements.

If you want something that lasts, you have to show up with more than affection. You need character. You need clarity. You need emotional discipline.

And let's talk about the conversations that are required for that foundation.

At some point, you're going to have to say hard things to the person you care about. That's non-negotiable. Avoiding the tough talks doesn't preserve a relationship—it sabotages it. When something is wrong and you remain silent, you choose resentment over resolution.

But there's a key difference between saying something hard and saying it harshly.

You can speak truth with love. You can be direct without being cruel. You can be firm and still be compassionate. And if you care about someone, you must learn to do exactly that. Because real connection is built in those moments—not the easy ones.

You want to build a bond that endures? Start by learning how to tell the truth without tearing each other down.

Now, what I'm about to say might throw you off for a second. It may feel like it's coming out of left field—but stay with me. It's going to make sense. I promise.

Let me ask you something, and I want you to answer honestly—not the version you give when someone else is watching.

How many times have you looked at your life and thought, "This is exactly where I want to be"?

Not where you're supposed to be. Not where your job, your degree, or your community thinks you should be. But where you actually want to be. Can you count those moments on one hand? Maybe not even that?

Now flip the question.

How many times have you looked at your life and realized you've been living a script that wasn't written by you?

The relationship that looks good on paper but feels hollow behind closed doors. The job that pays the bills but starves your soul. The love you settled for because it met society's criteria. You're checking all the boxes—but none of them were your boxes to begin with.

And here's the kicker: we often don't even recognize it until the discontent becomes unbearable.

Social media doesn't help. You scroll through your feed and see curated lives, perfect images, polished love stories—and you start believing that your life could be better, if only you had what they had. If only your spouse looked like that. If only you lived in another state. If only you had taken a different path. If only…

Let me stop you right there.

Who told you what your life should look like? Your parents? Your college advisor? The media? Some influencer who built their "truth" on filters and affiliate links?

Did you map out your career because it's what you wanted, or because your parents were footing the bill and their expectations came with a price tag? Did you fall into your profession or relationship out of design—or did you just drift there while trying to please everyone else?

These are the hard questions that too few people are willing to ask. But I'm going to challenge you to face them head-on.

Why do you care what anyone thinks of your life if they're not part of your inner circle? Why does the opinion of someone who doesn't invest in your peace, your growth, or your purpose get to influence your decisions?

Here's a truth most people don't want to hear: Society's rules weren't written for your fulfillment. They were written for conformity.

You're not here to live a life that looks acceptable—you're here to live a life that feels true.

And the only way to do that is to define your life and your relationship on your own terms.

I've seen people create something extraordinary with their spouse—not because it followed tradition, but because it worked for them. They stopped trying to impress the crowd and started building something real. They made their own rules. And their relationship flourished.

So let me say it clearly: To hell with what society expects. To hell with the fake guidelines, the filtered lives, the performative standards. This is your life. This is your relationship. And no one gets to tell you what it's supposed to look like unless they're waking up in your shoes and putting in the work beside you.

Live boldly. Love honestly. And if your truth doesn't fit their narrative? Let them choke on their expectations.

You don't owe anyone your conformity.

You owe yourself your freedom.

I once came across a video where a woman was asked, "Why don't you talk to your girlfriends about your relationship with your husband?" Her answer stopped me in my tracks. She said, "Why would I talk to the peasants about the king?"

Now that's the kind of mindset I respect.

Too many people run to their friends, siblings, or coworkers the moment something in their relationship doesn't feel right. Instead of going straight to the source—the person they actually have a problem with—they open the door to outside opinions, projections, and assumptions. And once that door is open, it's hard to close.

Let me be direct: the person you should be talking to is the one you're in the relationship with. Not your best friend. Not your cousin. Not your coworker over lunch. Them.

I use a simple principle in my coaching practice and in my own life:

Talk to them, not about them.

If you've got a problem with something they're doing—or not doing—why would you waste your time hashing it out with someone who has no context, no emotional investment, and no ability to actually fix it?

Your friends don't know the full story. They don't know how your spouse or significant other thinks. They don't know what values they hold or how deeply those values run. At best, they're guessing. At worst, they're projecting their own issues onto yours.

And that goes for both men and women. This isn't a gender issue. It's a maturity issue.

Both people in a relationship are equally responsible for clear, effective communication. That includes stating your needs. That includes setting boundaries. That includes being honest when something isn't working.

If you can't talk openly with the person you're with, you're not in a relationship—you're just two people pretending to be close while hiding behind emotional distance.

And that's why communication in the beginning is crucial. That's when you find out if you're choosing someone you can actually build with. Not someone who's just fun to be around—but someone you can resolve conflict with, someone you can grow alongside, and someone you can speak truth to without fear of fallout.

If you get that part right early, you'll avoid a world of problems later.

Let me ask you something most people never slow down long enough to consider:

Have you ever actually sat down and figured out what you want in a relationship?

I don't mean a vague wish list. I mean clear, non-negotiable standards that reflect the kind of person you're willing to build a life with.

Now let me push a little further:

Have you ever walked away from someone because they didn't meet those standards?

Not because of a bad day or a misunderstanding, but because your core values didn't align? Because their character clashed with your vision for the future?

Or are you nodding along, knowing full well you've stayed too long in situations where the red flags were waving like a parade?

Let's be clear: every relationship comes with expectations. You have a mental image of how you want your significant other to behave, believe, and communicate. Some of those expectations are flexible. Most aren't.

For example, maybe you have a preference for blonde women, but you meet someone with red hair who grabs your attention. That's probably not a deal-breaker—unless it is. But most people, if they're honest, can admit those preferences are surface-level. They don't belong on your non-negotiables list.

That list is reserved for things like character, values, morals, and how they handle communication.

I'll give you a personal example: being a strong communicator is high on my list. If I'm dealing with someone who shuts down, avoids the truth, or weaponizes silence, we're done before we start. Because communication isn't a luxury in a relationship—it's a lifeline.

Maybe for you, faith is critical. If you're a Christian and deeply rooted in that foundation, then dating someone who doesn't share that worldview might not be something you can live with. That's what we call a non-negotiable. And you need to identify it before you get emotionally entangled, not after.

But here's where most people screw this up.

They define their standards with statements like, "She just can't be bitchy," or "He better not be an asshole." Let me be honest with you—that tells me nothing. What does "bitchy" mean to you? What does "asshole" actually look like in behavior?

You've got to go deeper.

Maybe to you, an "asshole" is someone who's a staunch conservative. Maybe "bitchy" means you're describing a liberal who's vocal and assertive. Fair enough. But at least own it. Define it. Understand what bothers you and why.

Because until you spell out what matters most to you, you'll keep getting involved with people who look good on the outside but are fundamentally incompatible with the values that run your life.

This is not about being judgmental. It's about being intentional.

And once you start making compromises on those non-negotiables, it becomes a pattern. The more you bend early in the relationship, the more likely you are to keep bending in the future—and not in healthy ways. You'll silence your needs. You'll justify disrespect. You'll tolerate incompatibility. And then one day you'll wake up frustrated, burned out, and wondering how you got here.

Here's how: you ignored your own standards.

You chose comfort or chemistry over compatibility.

You thought you could mold them into what you wanted—or worse, that you could change them.

Let me save you some time: adults don't change unless they want to. And even then, it's rare. So, if someone's behavior, beliefs, or values clash with yours from the start, you've got two options:

Speak up and give them a shot to align with your expectations—if they're open to growth.

Walk away before the resentment takes root.

Either way, you protect your integrity.

So, here's your assignment:

Make a list of your non-negotiable standards. Not preferences. Not vague ideals. Concrete, character-based absolutes. And don't settle for anything less.

Because settling now means suffering later.

And the last thing you want is to look back on a broken relationship and realize you saw the problem from the start—you just ignored it.

Figure Out and Know What You Want

Taking the time to figure out what you really want might feel like an overwhelming process. You might even convince yourself it'll take too long, that it's too much work, or that it's easier to "see where things go." That mindset is exactly why so many people end up in the wrong relationship, wasting time, energy, and emotional bandwidth on people who were never aligned with their values in the first place.

Yes, it will take time. Yes, it might include some bad dates or false starts. But investing in clarity now will save you from chaos later. When you truly know what you want in a man or woman, you'll stop entertaining options that don't deserve your time. You'll stop confusing chemistry with compatibility. You'll stop negotiating your standards just to fill a void.

Let me remind you of something I've already said—and I'll say it again because it matters:

The relationship you choose will be the most important decision of your life.

This isn't just about romance. It's about alignment. It's about building a life with someone you trust to show up every day—when it's easy and especially when it's not. It's the person you'll turn to in crisis. The person you'll plan your future with. The one who helps you make life-altering decisions. If that foundation is unstable, everything else you build on top of it will eventually crack.

So here's the standard: you must be able to trust them. Not blindly. Not because you want to. But because they've earned that trust over time—through their behavior, their decisions, and their consistency.

But let's clear something up: trust is not about jumping through hoops to keep someone happy. It's not about appeasement or concession. You don't build trust by folding every time there's conflict or by sacrificing your voice to avoid rocking the boat.

Trust is built through repeated actions—when someone consistently chooses the relationship over their own ego. When their decisions reflect a genuine commitment to you, to the relationship, and to the long-term vision you share. It's not about perfection. It's about direction. Are they acting in your best interest? Are they choosing integrity when no one's watching? Are they protecting what you've built together?

That's trust.

But here's what's just as important—and what most people overlook:

You have to trust yourself first.

You have to trust your own judgment. You have to trust that your standards matter. You have to trust that if something doesn't feel right, it probably isn't. You have to trust your gut when it tells you a behavior is a red flag—even if your emotions are telling you to give it more time.

And when something crosses a line you've already defined as non-negotiable?

You don't rationalize it. You walk.

Society will feed you all kinds of messages. Some will tell you to be more tolerant. Others will tell you that your standards are too high. Some might pressure your significant other to behave in a way that contradicts what you need in a relationship.

None of that matters. What matters is this: Do their decisions align with your values? Are they making choices that make you feel respected, secure, and valued?

If the answer is no, don't silence yourself. Don't stay out of fear. Don't compromise out of loneliness. Because if you can't trust yourself to honor your standards, why should anyone else?

Know what you want.

Write it down.

Stand by it.

Because your future depends on it.

Now that you've put in the work to identify your non-negotiables, it's time to figure out the other side of the equation—what is negotiable.

But before we go any further, let me make one thing perfectly clear:

How someone treats you is not negotiable.

Read that again.

How someone talks to you, respects you, values you, shows up for you—that is not up for debate. If that's something you've mistakenly listed as flexible, go back right now and move it to the top of your non-negotiables list. Because if you allow someone to mistreat you, disrespect you, or violate your boundaries under the excuse of "no one's perfect," then you're setting the tone for every relationship that follows.

People will treat you the way you allow them to. And if you let disrespect slide once, it won't be the last time. Standards only work if you enforce them.

You deserve to be treated in a way that aligns with your values, your worth, and your vision for what a relationship should feel like. That's not entitlement. That's self-respect. Don't confuse the two.

Now, let's talk about what *is* negotiable.

This is where nuance matters. There are things about a person that might not be ideal, but they don't violate your core standards. You may not love every habit they have, but you can live with it. Maybe they're a little messy in the kitchen. Maybe they're not as outgoing as you are. Maybe they don't share your exact taste in music or how they unwind after a long day.

Here's the key: you need to know the difference between deal-breakers and differences.

Deal-breakers violate your values. Differences just require understanding.

Not every disagreement or quirk is a red flag. Relationships aren't built on perfection—they're built on compatibility, shared vision, and the ability to live with the parts of someone that don't trigger your boundaries.

You don't need to make a laundry list of every small annoyance. That'll drive you mad. But you do need to have a clear internal filter for what's okay and what isn't.

And here's where experience comes in. Sometimes, you won't know a particular behavior is a deal-breaker until you've dated someone who does it. Maybe you think something is minor until you realize it grinds your gears every single day. That's fine. When that happens—adjust your standards going forward. Take the lesson, add the behavior to your non-negotiables list, and move forward with more clarity.

Your standards are allowed to evolve.

But what you cannot do—what you must *never* do— is let someone consistently violate your peace, then convince yourself you're asking for too much. That's not compromise. That's self-abandonment.

So here's the challenge:

- Define what you can live with.
- Identify what you can't.
- And when you're unsure, always lean toward protecting your peace over preserving a relationship that makes you doubt yourself.

Because the more you tolerate what unsettles you, the more you'll erode your own confidence in the process.

So, how do you know if someone is truly who they say they are?

It starts with a simple but critical question: Do their actions align with their words? Are they consistent in what they say and how they behave—not just today, but over time? Not just when it's easy, but when it's inconvenient, stressful, or uncomfortable?

Anyone can present a version of themselves that looks ideal. That's what dating is. It's a highlight reel, not a documentary. But the goal isn't to be impressed by the presentation—it's to look behind the curtain and see if the substance matches the surface.

This is why vetting someone is not just important— it's vital.

Some people call it "testing." I call it paying attention. You're not manipulating them. You're observing them. You're trying to figure out if who they're presenting themselves as is really who they are—and whether you're truly compatible for the long haul.

That takes time. And it should. Making a long-term commitment based on a short-term impression is one of the fastest ways to end up in a miserable situation.

As you move through the relationship, ask yourself:

- Are they consistent?
- Do they follow through?
- Do they respect your boundaries without being reminded?
- Are they who they said they were when you met?

Also ask: Are you noticing red flags? If so, are those red flags truly about them—or are they projections of your own past wounds, insecurities, or unresolved experiences?

Not every uncomfortable feeling is a deal-breaker. But if something keeps pinging your gut, don't silence it. Trusting your instincts is part of trusting yourself. And when something crosses into non-negotiable territory, the decision should be immediate: walk away while you still can.

Don't overinvest in someone who's already shown you they're not aligned with what you need. The pain of leaving now is always less than the heartbreak of staying too long.

There's a quote that gets thrown around a lot, but few people take seriously:

"When someone shows you who they are, believe them."

Believe it. People rarely change at their core. They may evolve in some areas, sure—but their fundamental values, behaviors, and patterns tend to stay the same. If someone shows you something about themselves that you know is incompatible with who you are or what you need—don't try to fix them. Don't wait for them to evolve. Just move on.

You're not asking them to change. You're making a decision to not build a future with someone who doesn't respect your boundaries or align with your standards. And honestly—why would you want to be with someone who has to change who they are just to be with you?

That's not love. That's manipulation in disguise.

You may have heard the phrase, "The right person will change for you." Let me say this flat-out: That's nonsense.

The right person won't need to change.

They will already meet your standards. They will already respect your boundaries. They will already align with your values. You won't need to reshape them into who you need—they'll already show up as that person.

That's not controlling. That's clarity.

Which brings us to a public example that deserves a serious reality check: Jonah Hill.

He was dragged through the social media mud after his ex-girlfriend posted screenshots of messages where Jonah laid out his expectations in the relationship. He said, essentially, "You're free to live however you want. But here are the things I will not accept in someone I'm dating. If those are things you want to continue doing, we're not a fit."

And for that, he was labeled controlling. The media pounced. The comment section turned into a dumpster fire of people—many of whom call themselves feminists—claiming he was trying to "own" her.

Let's stop the nonsense.

What Jonah did was set boundaries. Clear ones.

He said, "This is who I am. These are the standards I live by. If you want to live differently, that's your right. But I'm not the guy for you." That's not controlling. That's healthy communication. That's emotional maturity. That's how adults operate.

Now, could she have boundaries and expectations of her own? Absolutely. Maybe she did. But she didn't post those. She chose to publicize his, likely hoping for validation. What she got instead was a parade of people applauding her for rejecting what they saw as "controlling," when in reality, it was just a man stating his terms clearly.

Here's what people forget: boundaries are not ultimatums. They're filters.

You're not saying, "Do this or else." You're saying, "This is what I will or won't accept. If that doesn't work for you, we're simply not a match."

That's fair. That's respectful. That's necessary.

And if someone can't handle your boundaries, your expectations, or your standards—they are free to walk away.

But they don't get to shame you for having them.

So let me end this section with the truth that most won't say out loud:

They can be who they are. You just don't have to let them be that person with you.

That's not unfair.

That's freedom—for both of you.

Protecting your peace at the start of a relationship is not a flaw—it's a necessity.

People throw around words like "selfish" or "guarded" as if safeguarding your emotional well-being is something to be ashamed of. It's not. In fact, it's one of the most important things you can do to build a relationship that's functional, respectful, and sustainable.

Boundaries are not barriers. They're markers of mutual respect. When you respect someone else's boundaries, you're saying, I care enough about you to be mindful of how my behavior impacts you. You're showing them they matter—not just in your life, but in your decisions.

That goes both ways. Everyone in a relationship has the right to have boundaries, expectations, and standards— and both people are equally responsible for honoring them. Respect doesn't just mean love. It means creating a space where the other person feels safe, heard, and considered.

And here's a reality check—if someone has a boundary you can't respect, that person isn't for you. That's not cruelty. That's clarity. It's better to walk away early than to stick around hoping the discomfort will fade or convincing them to "ease up." That's not fair to them, and frankly, it's not fair to you either.

Breaking up isn't easy. Especially when feelings are involved, or when lives are starting to intertwine. But ending things early—before too much time, energy, or emotion has been invested—is often the most respectful thing you can do. Trying to shift someone's boundary to make them easier to date? That's not compromise. That's manipulation.

The goal of a relationship is not to turn someone into what you want. It's to find someone who already lives within the values you've chosen to build your life around.

Now, let's talk about authenticity—because that's where this conversation gets real.

We live in a time where authenticity is both in high demand and short supply. People don't always show up as who they really are. They present the polished version. The curated version. The "safe" version. And they'll keep that mask on for as long as it takes to make you commit.

You've probably heard the excuse before: "No one can wear a mask forever." That sounds great until you meet someone who manages to wear it just long enough to get what they want.

I've heard from men who dated women for years—engaged, living together—only to watch the entire personality shift once the ring was on her finger. But let's be fair: this cuts both ways. There are plenty of women who experience the same bait-and-switch from men once the emotional leverage is in place.

Sometimes this behavior is rooted in fear. People worry that if they show who they really are, they'll be rejected. So they delay the truth. They fake alignment. They pretend to be more agreeable, more accommodating, more "ideal" than they really are—just long enough to earn your loyalty.

Other times? It's manipulation. Plain and simple.

Whatever the reason, the outcome is the same: you're now committed to someone who isn't who they originally claimed to be.

That's why the vetting process matters. That's why time, consistency, and clarity are your best allies in making sure you're not signing up for a role in someone else's performance.

Here's what you need to remember:

- If something feels off, it probably is.
- If you find yourself confused by their behavior, trust your gut.
- If their words sound right but their actions don't line up, pay attention.

You're not responsible for making someone change. And they're not obligated to become someone they're not just to stay in your life.

When the match doesn't fit, that's your cue to leave. You're not being cold—you're being honest. They can still be who they are, just not with you. And there's nothing unfair about that.

In fact, that's one of the most respectful decisions you can make—for them and for yourself.

Having boundaries doesn't mean you're selfish. It doesn't mean you don't care about the other person. What it *does* mean is that you have enough self-respect to protect your peace, your values, and your emotional well-being.

That's not a weakness. That's emotional maturity.

Too often, we hesitate to enforce boundaries because we're afraid it'll make someone uncomfortable. We worry we're being too rigid, or we'll push them away, or we'll come off as controlling. But here's what really happens when you fail to draw the line: you don't just disappoint yourself—you slowly begin to lose yourself.

Every time you let a personal boundary be crossed, you chip away at your self-worth. You compromise your values. You silence your inner voice. And with each repetition, the resentment builds—toward them and toward yourself.

Eventually, it shows up in your relationship like this:

- You feel tension every time they repeat the same behavior.
- You start blaming them for not respecting you.
- You start blaming yourself for not standing up sooner.

And by the time the emotional damage is done, it's not about that one boundary anymore—it's about the long-term erosion of your self-esteem. The relationship becomes a breeding ground for frustration, distance, and silent resentment. And worst of all, you look back and realize you let it happen.

I've said it before: the relationship was doomed from the beginning because you kept letting things slide.

Had you drawn that line early—clearly and unapologetically—you would've either seen them adjust out of genuine respect, or you would've had the clarity to walk away. Either outcome would've saved you from the slow burn of self-betrayal.

And here's what matters most: when you stand by your boundaries, your self-respect remains intact—even if the relationship ends.

Yes, there's give-and-take in every healthy relationship. Yes, there are sacrifices worth making. But let's be crystal clear: your self-respect is never one of them. Neither is your peace. Neither is your dignity.

You don't excuse repeated boundary violations under the banner of "compromise." That's not compromise. That's self-neglect.

Take Jonah Hill's example. I don't know the man personally, but I saw what he did—and from where I'm sitting, it was healthy. He laid out what he couldn't tolerate in a relationship. He expressed clearly and calmly what would disrupt his peace, undermine his values, and ultimately harm his self-worth.

He didn't demand that the other person change. He didn't issue ultimatums. He simply said, "This is what I expect in a relationship. If that's not aligned with you, we're not a match."

That's not control. That's clarity with respect.

He gave her the freedom to continue doing whatever she wanted. He just made it clear that those choices wouldn't exist within a relationship with him. And that's exactly how it should be—not just in romantic relationships, but in every relationship worth keeping.

So here's the bottom line:

Let people be who they are—but don't betray who *you* are just to keep them.

If someone's actions are hurting you, conflicting with your values, or crossing the lines you've drawn for your emotional safety, it's not your job to convince them to change. It's your responsibility to walk away with your integrity intact.

Ending something doesn't mean it was all a mistake. It just means you've reached a point where continuing would require sacrificing the very things that make you whole.

And as I've said before, many things in life are simple, but not easy. Don't confuse the two. Protecting your peace is simple. Enforcing your standards is simple. Walking away when someone doesn't align with your truth is simple.

But no, it's not easy.

Still, it's the most important thing you can do for your future. Because on the other side of self-respect is clarity. On the other side of boundaries is peace. And on the other side of walking away is the freedom to find someone who truly sees you—and respects you from the start.

That is what you deserve.

And that's the standard you set when you stop settling.

Chapter 10:
The Wake-Up Call I Didn't Ask For
(But Damn Well Needed)

"The world will ask you who you are, and if you don't know, the world will tell you."

- Carl Jung

This past year has been a whirlwind. So many moving parts, so many things shifting at once—including writing this book—that I honestly can't even explain what it feels like to be nearing the finish line. There's excitement. There's uncertainty. There's that whisper of fear that comes when you're about to release something raw and real into the world, not knowing if it'll be accepted, rejected, praised, or ripped apart. All of it's on the table—and I'm not going to pretend I'm not scared. Releasing this book scares the absolute shit out of me.

And not for the reasons most people think.

It's not the criticism that keeps me up at night. It's the fact that I almost didn't make it here at all. Literally. I almost died.

Back in January, just as I started a regular gym session, I had a massive heart attack. No warning. No lead-up. Just pain and then the scramble to get to the hospital. Within 15 minutes of arriving at the ER, I went into cardiac arrest. I don't remember everything, but I remember enough to understand that everything had to go exactly right for me to still be breathing today. The right place. The right time. The right people. And I got lucky.

That's not a story I tell for sympathy. That's a story I tell because it gave me the kind of clarity you can't buy in any book or find on a podcast. It forced me to stop bullshitting myself and start living with more purpose, more honesty, and more fire than I ever have.

I've got nothing but gratitude for the people who stepped in that day. And for the woman who showed up for me afterward—you know who you are—your care during that recovery reminded me what real presence looks like. It's because of people like you that I hold myself to a higher standard now. I owe it to the people who love me, and to myself, to show up as the best version of me. Every damn day. Even on the days I fall short.

I'll be honest—I had already figured out a lot of what's in this book before the heart attack. But the heart attack? That sharpened everything. It clarified what I want out of life, what kind of legacy I want to leave my children, and how I want to show up in the world. Writing this book took me a long time, and the break I had to take for recovery stretched it even further. The CPR and shocks left me with injuries that made even sitting down at a desk a battle some days. But here's the truth: I never once thought about quitting. I've seen people lie in bed, let life steamroll them, and give up. I've seen what surrender looks like. And that ain't me.

I don't wear my recovery like a badge of honor. I credit my stubbornness, a world-class medical team, and the fierce love of the people around me. But I also know this—life tried to take me out, and I didn't fold. That counts for something.

Now, I'm working with a trainer again, getting my body back in shape. I feel stronger, clearer, and more locked in than I've ever been. I've still got more to say—especially to the men, which is why I'm already planning the next book—but this one right here? This one had to come first.

This book is my heartbeat on paper. I didn't write it just to vent. I wrote it because I lived it. Because I almost didn't get to finish it. And because someone out there needs to hear that your pain, your wake-up call, your "almost didn't make it"—can be the very thing that wakes you up to everything that still matters.

Let me be clear—I'm not telling you my story just to hear myself talk. I'm telling it because there's purpose in it. And if I've got one, then so do you.

You can change your life. Full stop. I don't care who told you otherwise. You can learn new skills, shift your mindset, start over, or rebuild from scratch. You just have to decide that your life is worth that kind of effort—and then commit to doing the work.

I'm not the greatest writer in the world. I won't pretend to be. But I've got a solid-ass team behind me who believed in this book, helped me shape it, and made sure it stayed aligned with what I actually wanted to say. That's the point—you don't have to have all the answers. You just have to decide you're willing to find them.

We live in an age where anything you want to learn is just a few clicks away. The information is there. The how-to videos. The coaching. The books. The forums. The answers. But none of that means a damn thing if you're not willing to choose the harder path and start climbing.

Now, I know what you're thinking—"That sounds too simple." And you're right, it is. The decision to change your life is the easy part. It's everything after that that's hard. The failures. The long nights. The uncertainty. The days when it feels like nothing you're doing is making a difference.

That's the part most people run from. But I'm here to tell you—failing isn't the problem. Quitting is.

You're going to fall. You're going to screw up. You're going to doubt whether you're cut out for this. And when that happens, you have two choices: fold or get back up. Dust yourself off. Take a breath. And go again.

That's what I had to do after my heart attack. I had a choice—live or die. And I don't mean physically. I'm talking about giving up on life, going into hiding, playing it safe, and letting fear and pain dictate the rest of my days. I could have become a ghost of myself, wallowing in self-pity and convincing myself the fight wasn't worth it.

But I chose differently. And so can you.

Whatever you're facing—whether it's a broken relationship, a failed attempt at love, a job you hate, or a mountain of self-doubt—you have to choose to keep playing the game of life. You have to decide you're still in it. That you're still building. That your story isn't over.

No one's coming to save you. Despite what Jelly Roll sings about, that rescue isn't happening. No cavalry. No hero. No miracle fix. You have to save yourself.

Sure, people may throw you a rope. Some will show up to lend a hand or give you encouragement. But you still have to grab that rope and climb. You still have to put one foot in front of the other. You still have to choose to conquer your life—regardless of how high the climb is or how many times you've slipped before.

You're your own lifeline. So act like it.

If you're going to build anything meaningful in this life—especially when it comes to relationships—you've got to be open. Open to being wrong. Open to seeing yourself clearly, even when it's uncomfortable. Open to learning hard truths and accepting that someone else's perspective might hold weight.

That includes everything I've written in this book. Don't just take my word for it—think critically. Let it challenge you. Do your own digging, ask your own questions, and come to your own conclusions. But don't close the door on ideas just because they make you squirm.

I've come to a conclusion of my own: we can't afford to let the division between men and women become a permanent reality. It's manufactured, and it's destructive. We weren't created to be enemies. We were designed to connect, to build something together, to bring out the best in each other. That's not some feel-good cliché—it's the truth. We're wired for it. Look at biology. Look at psychology. Look at the way we complement one another when we're at our best. It's undeniable.

This book isn't about theory—it's about behavior. It's about the patterns you've built, the stories you tell yourself, and how those things shape how you treat the opposite sex.

Ask yourself: how do you behave toward them? Is it respectful? Is it defensive? Is it shaped by bad advice, bitterness, or someone else's baggage? Maybe you had a terrible experience with someone who did you wrong. I get it. That pain is real, and it doesn't just disappear overnight. But that one person—or even a few—doesn't get to define every man or every woman you'll meet for the rest of your life. That's on you.

You can't let bad actors poison your future. You can't let hurt close you off to the possibility of something incredible with someone who actually fits you. That kind of pessimism becomes a prison—and it's self-imposed.

Now, here's the part nobody wants to hear: you're not perfect. Not as a man. Not as a woman. You're going to mess up. You're going to say the wrong thing. You're going to hurt someone, even when you don't mean to. And guess what? So will the person you're with.

That's the reality of human relationships. They're messy, imperfect, and full of moments where you'll be tested. Things go sideways. Emotions flare. Disagreements happen. But that's not a reason to shut down or give up on people entirely.

You keep going. You get wiser. You learn what really matters to you and what doesn't. You stop chasing perfection and start focusing on consistency, integrity, and respect.

Because honestly? Hating the opposite sex is exhausting. Carrying that kind of bitterness? It drains you. It eats up your time, your energy, and your peace of mind. And for what? So you can win arguments no one's keeping score on?

Let that shit go. You're not meant to walk through life bitter and guarded. You're meant to live. To connect. To grow. And that means staying open—especially when it's hard.

Look, we all have things that piss us off—things we dislike, hate, or flat-out loathe. I've laid out plenty of them throughout this book. But here's the difference: I'm not dumping that energy into bitterness. I'm putting it toward change. Toward calling out what's broken and offering a better way to think, especially when it comes to how men and women view each other.

This book isn't some anti-woman manifesto. It's not about hating men, either. It's about calling both sides to a higher standard. If we're being honest—really honest—we'd probably agree that both men and women have room to improve. But we also have to acknowledge that life is messy. People are flawed. Mistakes happen. Still, society keeps pumping out a narrative that says men and women are enemies—and that narrative is tearing us apart.

We've got to shut that down. Because the truth is, masculinity has taken a serious hit. We live in a gynocentric culture that treats masculinity like it's a problem to be solved. But masculinity, in its truest form, is not toxic. It's necessary. And deep down, most people—men and women—know that.

Are there toxic men out there? Absolutely. But toxicity isn't masculinity. Toxicity is just toxicity. The same way there are toxic women who get labeled as "strong" or "independent" when they're really just manipulative and selfish. But no one's rushing to call femininity toxic, right?

The truth is, some of you just had the bad luck of running into a few toxic men. It happens. But that doesn't make all men dangerous or masculinity itself a threat.

Misogynists exist, sure—but not in the numbers the media or modern feminists want you to believe. Most men are just trying to do their best and figure things out, same as anyone else.

Let's get clear about this: masculinity looks like strength with restraint, courage with compassion, discipline with purpose, and presence without ego. It's responsibility. It's consistency. It's standing firm when life gets hard and not folding under pressure. That's what real masculinity is. It's not loud, it's not reckless, and it sure as hell isn't abusive. It's measured. It's intentional. And when it's healthy, it's powerful in all the right ways.

Now let's talk about the feminine. Feminine energy, at its core, is one of the most beautiful forces on earth. Nurturing, intuitive, emotionally intelligent, and life-giving. But modern feminism didn't just warp masculinity—it went after femininity too. And it wasn't men who did that. It was women, selling each other the lie that softness is weakness, that emotional expression is a flaw, that interdependence is oppressive.

What started as a legitimate push for equal rights has mutated into a cultural machine that now shames men for existing, dismisses responsibility, and rewards victimhood. The language has shifted from enablement to entitlement. Words like "patriarchy," "weaponized incompetence," and "toxic masculinity" are thrown around so casually they've lost all meaning. It's no longer about progress. It's about blame. It's about power. And in the process, it's turned many women against men—and against their own feminine nature.

Let me be crystal clear: I don't support the men who hate women either. That's just the flip side of the same broken coin. Both stances are lazy. They're cop-outs.

They're ways of avoiding responsibility and living in blame instead of ownership.

We're in 2025. If you're still pointing fingers at someone else for your life's problems, you're wasting time. No more blaming your ex, your parents, or the system. It's on you now. And yes, the system has flaws. But personal accountability? That's your job.

We've got to stop playing into the division that's being fed to us. It's profitable for the loudest voices, but it's poison for the rest of us. Use some damn common sense. See people for who they are—not just the label society tells you they represent. We need peace between men and women, not war.

Are there bad actors on both sides? No question. But let's stop pretending they represent all of us.

Both men and women can do better—and should. That's not an attack. That's a challenge. Because here's the truth: we all have standards. And every individual, man or woman, has the right to decide what they want in someone they're going to build a life with. It might not always feel fair, but it's real.

Maybe someone passed on you because you're overweight. Or because of your political views, your personal style, your habits, your beliefs, your insecurities. Maybe it's your greasy hair, the way you walk, or the fact that you're still figuring your life out. It could be anything. The point is—people are allowed to have preferences. Just like *you* have yours.

The key is not to take rejection as some ultimate judgment of your worth. Instead, ask yourself: Is there something I can do better? If there is, go do it. Improve your health. Clean up your appearance. Work on your mindset. But don't do it just to win someone over—do it because it makes you a better version of yourself. The kind of person that attracts someone naturally aligned with who you are.

Or maybe you decide not to change a thing—and that's fine too. Just don't sit around bitter because someone didn't choose you. That's not their problem. That's on you.

Men and women are not the same. And we don't have to be. That doesn't mean one is better than the other. It means we're different. Equal in value? Absolutely. Equal in purpose? Yes. But not equal in the sense of being interchangeable. We were built with different roles, traits, strengths, and energies. If we were all the same, this world wouldn't function. It literally couldn't.

We need each other. And when that's understood and respected, the dynamic becomes powerful.

Relationships only work when you know who you are. What you want. What you bring. What you're willing to tolerate—and what you're not. You need to pour into a relationship from day one, not wait until it starts falling apart. That's how you avoid messiness later.

Ask yourself: What are my standards? What am I about? What do I expect from someone I'm building a life with? If you haven't done that work, then you're winging it. And that's no way to create something real.

Even people who are polar opposites can make it work. You might be into loud music and sports. She might be into yoga and classical piano. Doesn't matter. If you share core values—respect, loyalty, ambition, faith, honesty—you can build something solid. It's the little stuff that can be negotiated.

Like how she slurps her coffee every morning. Annoying? Maybe. But if that's the biggest issue in your relationship, you're winning.

In this day and age, with all the noise coming from every direction, you've got to think for yourself. The media, the algorithms, the social platforms—they're all pushing an agenda, and most of the time, it's to keep men and women at odds. It's intentional. Division sells. Outrage gets clicks. But you're smarter than that.

You have to step outside the box and stop letting society tell you what kind of life you should have, who you should be with, or what kind of relationship is "normal." The truth is, most of what you're seeing out there is curated garbage. Half of it is bad information, and the other half isn't even real. It's manufactured conflict, manipulated statistics, and emotionally charged narratives meant to make you question what used to be common sense.

My advice? Tune it out.

Seriously—cut it off and focus on what's real in your life. The people around you. The way you treat others. The way you handle adversity. The values you stand on. That's what matters. Not some influencer's opinion or a Twitter thread full of misery and projection. None of that is helping you build anything real.

Stick to what's tangible. Stick to what brings peace. And let that peace guide you in how you deal with the opposite sex, how you show up in relationships, and how you live your damn life.

Use your head. Use your heart. And above all—use your own judgment.